THE CHF COUNTESS

A VALOR OF VINEHILL NOVEL

K.J. JACKSON

First Edition: July 2023
ISBN: 978-1-940149-85-1

K.J. JACKSON BOOKS

Historical Romance:

Hold Your Breath
Stone Devil Duke
Unmasking the Marquess
My Captain, My Earl

Lords of Fate
Worth of a Duke
Earl of Destiny
Marquess of Fortune

Lords of Action
Vow
Promise
Oath

Revelry's Tempest
Of Valor & Vice
Of Sin & Sanctuary
Of Risk & Redemption
To Capture a Rogue, *Logan's Legends*
To Capture a Warrior, *Logan's Legends*
The Devil in the Duke

Valor of Vinehill
The Iron Earl
The Wolf Duke
The Steel Rogue
The Christmas Countess
The Devil Baron

Box of Draupnir
The Heart of an Earl
The Blood of a Baron
The Soul of a Rogue

Exile
Exiled Duke
Wicked Exile
Dangerous Exile

Guardians of the Bones
Discreet Destruction
Shadows of Scandal
A Savage Deception
Wicked Reckoning

Paranormal Romance:
Creatures of Scales & Savagery
The Way You Break
Tear the World Down
Heathens in the Shadows
A Dynasty of Death

Contemporary Romance:

A Beautiful Average

Be sure to sign up for news of my next releases at
www.KJJackson.com

DEDICATION

– As Always,
For my favorite Ks

{ CHAPTER 1 }

She was sinking now. Sinking up to her knees.

Every step her feet descended deeper into the fluffy, bitter torture—the snow crusting about the top edges of her boots, rings of ice around her calves.

One more step.

It had to be only one more step.

When Karta had set out into the storm after the barn door wouldn't open for the drift in front of it, there'd still been daylight cutting through the greyness of the thick clouds blanketing the land with freezing snow.

It had seemed possible.

Make it to Kirkmere Abbey. It was only an hour walk on a sunny day.

Maggie's life depended upon her making it there.

But now…

Karta's look shifted up from the undulating waves of snow, searching through the pellets of ice searing into her skin—each one a freezing pinprick. An eerie white glow from the moon had taken over the land as the snow had stopped falling from the sky, but now the wind whipped across the glen, vicious, blinding her to her own hand in front of her face.

If she could just make it to the woodlands that lined the eastern border of Kirkmere land, the wind would be

broken. Broken enough for her to see the path again. Broken enough that her legs could move through the snow without battling the drifts that made every muscle in her body scream against the torture.

Keep forward.

The only choice now. She'd gone too far to even consider turning around and trying to make it back to the dower house. Death was surely waiting if she tried to retrace her footsteps through the drifts.

Her breathing had been slight ever since she'd stepped out into the howling winds, afraid to let the freezing air too deeply into her lungs. But exhaustion had set into her muscles and she needed air.

Real air.

Needed to stop her head from swaying.

She sucked in a gulp of frigid air. It chilled her from the inside out, the cold seeping even deeper into the marrow of her bones.

Keep forward.

The only option.

She tucked her chin back down, sinking it behind the edge of the wool cloak she held clasped at her neck and she tugged the edge of the hood far over her forehead.

Thirty more steps—each one a struggle as the snow devoured her legs, holding tight to her feet as she tried to lift them from the heavy drifts—and she felt no farther along than she had been minutes ago.

She stopped, hunched over against the bitter wind and gasping for air. Her breath now so cold it no longer puffed into cloud crystals as she exhaled. Each muscle in her body railed against her, demanding she yield, demanding she stop. Lie down.

Maggie. Maggie was dying. There was no time to stop.

With a screech, she yanked her right foot from the bank of snow it was wedged in. Five more steps and her shoulder knocked into a tree she didn't see.

The forest.

Almost there.

She just had to make it through a hundred yards of woods and then across the sheep fields and help would be at hand.

Her hand lifted from deep within the thick folds of her cloak, her fingers clutching the bark of the tree through her leather gloves. The forest would guide her. It had to.

Keep forward.

{ CHAPTER 2 }

Domnall Greyford muttered incoherent blasphemies under his breath as he walked to the east side door of Kirkmere Abbey. "Blasted pup, you couldn't take care of this on the journey here?"

He looked down at his favorite deerhound. No longer a pup, Theodora was full grown now, the wiry grey hairs atop her head reaching the middle of his thigh. Though for how tall he was, she was equally tall among her breed.

She whined again, looking insistently from him to the door. He didn't move quick enough and she nudged her nose under his hand.

Shaking his head, he opened the door. They'd just spent the last four hours making their way through the snowstorm to get to the abbey and he hadn't even taken his greatcoat off. Somewhere in that time, Theodora could have stopped to do her business.

The deerhound took off into the eerie white of the snow under the moon. She bounded through the tall drifts, her long legs and compact body only slightly hindered by the banks of snow. The bitter wind had died down, no longer blinding the land, though sudden gusts of whirling snow still danced over the fields.

Theodora kept going. And going.

Directly away from the abbey.

"Theodora."

He whistled.

She kept moving away, turning into a dark spec bouncing along the white blanket of snow.

"Little bugger." The last thing he wanted was to go back out into the blasted cold. They'd only just made it here.

He looked over his shoulder with a sigh. It wasn't as though it was any warmer in the abbey.

Two days from Christmastide, most of the staff had left the abbey to celebrate with their families. Only the head butler, the housekeeper, and the cook had stayed in residence.

Not that he minded.

He'd not sent word that he was arriving and he'd rather the employees enjoy the days away—the last thing he wanted with his new staff was to ruin their Christmastide. The only issue upon his arrival with three of his men was that there were only two fires burning in the abbey, and both were in the servants' quarters.

It would take some time for his men to get the fires lit and for warmth to eke back into several of the main rooms.

Domnall stuck his head out the door, took a deep breath, and sent a long piercing whistle into the land. Theodora always came to that whistle. Always.

His eyes scanned the white terrain under the glow of the moon.

Nothing.

He whistled again.

Barking.

Short yippy barks, echoing over the fields. Like nothing he'd ever heard from the deerhound.

"Damn." She hadn't injured herself, had she? The dog liked trouble, or trouble liked her—he was never quite sure which flip of the coin fate intended on that score.

If she hadn't endeared herself to him when she was a pup, he wouldn't be so quick to save her from scrape after scrape. Years ago, while her littermates would crowd his legs demanding his attention, she would sit to the side, staring at him, not sinking to their level with their desperate yaps for attention. No, Theodora was always one to wait—regal—until he came to her, tossed her the prime bone or scuffed her ears. But she was also loyal like no other—never one to stray from his heel when the other dogs would run off in a pack, frenzied in a hunt for a squirrel or a rabbit.

He would—to his own disgust at times—do anything for that hound.

His heartbeat quickened and Domnall stepped out of the abbey. Damn that he'd set his gloves down on a table in the foyer. But he didn't want to lose her in the snow if the moon decided to hide behind cloud cover, so he closed the door behind him, tucked his hands up into the sleeves of his greatcoat, and crunched into the first drift of snow. It reached up past his shins, just below his knees. Deeper than he'd thought it was. The horses had been champions earlier, trudging through the drifts with steadfast endurance.

The barking stopped and he whistled again.

The barks resumed.

He saw Theodora running toward him, leaping over the banks of snow. Good. Not injured.

He waited for her, another whistle poised on his lips if she thought to go rogue again.

A hundred paces away from him, she jerked to a stop, her short yippy barks firing into the air.

Barks, then she twisted in the snow, jumping high over a drift and running away from him again.

"Bloody mutt." He pulled the lapels of his overcoat tight up against his chin and trudged forward. He would throttle the hound once he got a hold of her.

It wasn't until he'd trudged—with every step requiring him to heave his legs up high to gain just a half foot—halfway across the field that led out to the east of the abbey that he realized he was doing exactly what Theodora wanted him to do.

Follow her.

He'd thought he'd been chasing the miscreant—a fun game for her and no one else—but after the fourth time she turned around, coming back for him and then ran away through the snow in front of him, he realized she was leading him.

Three quarters of the way across the field, Theodora stopped, barking, her wiry head popping up and down behind a drift to make sure he was still following.

He sped up his steps in her tracks.

His breath coming in pants for the exertion of plodding through the snow, he reached the last tall drift ten paces away from his hound.

He saw it.

Under the moonlight, a dark lump half buried in the snow. Theodora licking, her snout jabbed deep into the folds of the cape.

Domnall barreled his way through the last drift, sending snow flying.

A dark cloak covered the body, the head. A woman curled into a ball on her side. He bent over, brushing snow away from her shoulder and he rolled her onto her back.

Her body moved easily, not stiff. Possibly not even dead.

Theodora looked up at him and barked.

He nodded to the hound and looked down. His frozen fingers cracking as he bent them into motion, he shifted the hood of the cloak away from her face to set his hand at her nose to feel for breath.

Hell.

A face he recognized. A face he would always recognize, even under a sliver of moonlight.

No. Impossible. It couldn't be.

But it was.

His hands fumbling through the folds of her cape, he found her shoulders and gripped them, shaking her. Too hard, he knew. But she couldn't be dead. No.

He shook her again.

Her eyelashes crusted over with ice, she didn't open her eyes. But her hand lifted, searching until she found the sturdiness of his arm and grabbed it with all her might, weak as it was.

Her mouth opened, her voice raw wisps. The wind howling through the trees just beyond them drowned whatever sound escaped her lips.

"What? Tell me again." He leaned down close to her mouth, his ear next to her lips.

"Mag—Maggie—m—m—maid. Dying." Her words stuttered as she gasped a breath that shook her whole body. "Everyone's g—gone at the Leviton dower h—h—house. Doc—doctor. She needs a doctor. Send a doc..."

Her last words drifted into nothing.

Her hand fell from his arm, her body giving up.

For one long breath he was frozen in time, frozen above her, unable to move for the horror of finding her here like this.

Theodora barked, nudging her cold nose into his neck.

He sucked in a breath and bent over. Sliding his hands deep into the snow under her legs and back, he picked her up, clutching her to his body.

"I got ye, Karta. I got ye."

{ CHAPTER 3 }

Her feet. Warmth pressing into them. Heat where there was none. So stark against the cold her muscles revolted, pain shooting through them until the warmth overcame.

Again and again, the flesh of her feet bending, twisting into the swaddle of heat.

The sensation so odd, it pulled her mind from the blackness that had ensconced it.

Fire was near her. Warmth on her left cheek. The scent of smoke filling her nostrils.

Heaviness on her body, weighing her down—her arms, her torso, her thighs. But not her feet. Her feet were in the air.

Karta opened her eyes, instantly realizing that the ice that had formed on her lashes was now gone. The cold was gone. It had set deep into her bones, still freezing her from the inside out, but all around her was heat. Not cold.

Her eyes blurry for a moment, she had to concentrate hard on the figure by her feet. She squinted, her vision clearing with several blinks.

No. Not possible.

She squinted harder, the bright white of his lawn shirt hurting her eyes for the darkness they had just been drowning in.

"Dom?"

The head on the figure turned to her. "Aye."

His voice.

But he couldn't be real. She glanced around her. Fire to her left. The back of a long, blue upholstered settee to her right. Hefty wooden beams above her. Layers of heavy blankets atop her—too many to count. She wasn't at the dower house.

Domnall's hands—his hands on her bare feet were causing the most oddly wonderful sensations about her toes.

A dream. This was a dream.

A dream she wanted to stay in.

Or maybe a nightmare.

Her gaze landed on him. "Are you real or is this a dream?"

"Real, lass."

Her look drifted from him to stare at the white plaster between the heavy beams above. What sort of cruel world had she fallen into where she was alive in front of a fire with the one man—of all the countless people in the world— that had broken her heart long ago?

A man she hated.

She stifled the urge to yank her feet from his hands. Not that she could move a muscle at the moment.

Calm.

She needed calm. Needed to figure out what was happening.

She drew in a shaky breath. "We are at Kirkmere Abbey?"

"Aye."

"I made it?"

"Ye had a spot of help from Theodora."

Her look dropped to him, her brow wrinkling. "Theodora?" She cleared her throat, trying to not let her voice squeak. "Your wife?"

"My hound." He inclined his head to the deerhound curled next to the hearth, its big black eyes open and watchful on them, even as it had nestled close into the lazy comfort of the fire.

She closed her eyes, trying to remember the last thing she could before the blackness had taken over. The cold. The cold all around her, her hand left the tree and she lost her anchor—adrift in the endless snow—with the wind whipping at her eyes until she could no longer see. No longer think. The last shreds of her hope that she was travelling in the right direction disappearing. Spinning in a circle, she dropped. Dropped into the comfort of the snow. The soft embrace of it. Then darkness. What had she been doing?

Hell.

Her look whipped to Domnall. "Maggie—Maggie— my maid, she's—"

"She's sick. Ye told me. I sent one of my men to fetch the physician and two to fetch Maggie."

"They're bringing her here?"

"Aye. Ye said there was no one there—or at least there better not be, for why else would ye get it into yer fool head to walk into a snowstorm that had whited out the sky."

The warmth of his low brogue wrapped around her. Calm. Even as he was scolding her.

She shook her head, her chin rubbing along the blankets tucked around her neck. "There isn't. It was just us—the rest of the staff is gone for Christmastide."

His fingers rubbing her feet stopped and he looked away. His jaw shifted, tensed, just like it always had years ago when he was beyond irate with her.

So much for calm.

She studied his profile. He had the dark scruff of a week's worth of a beard covering his face, blending up along his cheek into his light brown hair. His dark blue eyes—the color of her deepest indigo dress—were set solidly on the crackling fire four feet to her left. Crinkles of lines around his eyes made him look older. Older than when she'd last seen him six years past.

He wore only a lawn shirt, and at that, he still looked hot. The blazing fire wasn't helping with that. Had he always been this big, this strong? Or was it that she'd been surrounded by small, thin men for too long?

His head turned to her, his dark blue eyes pinning her. "What the blasted hell were ye doing going out into that storm, Karta?"

"I wasn't about to let Maggie die. I was of no help to her—the only thing I could do was come for help."

"So you'd have both of ye dead instead of just one of ye? A fool's mission that was."

"Dom—"

"Why didn't ye take a horse?" His hand clamped onto her right foot and squeezed it. Hard, but for how the touch seared heat into her, she'd take it.

"I may be a fool but I'm not an idiot." She met his glare, the indignant fire in her chest warming her more than the blankets. "I went to the stable first to get a mare, but the snow had drifted in front of the doors and I couldn't get them open more than a crack. Not enough for me to even get into the barn. I thought there was enough time to get here before nightfall. The snow was easing, but then the wind came up when I was only a quarter of the way here. It blinded me. But I thought I could still make it."

"You were always too stubborn." The words grumbled, he tore his gaze away from her, his look landing on the fire. His fingers started massaging her feet on his lap again.

Heaven. Absolute heaven, even if her bones felt like ice.

For this, she could set her hatred of him aside for the moment.

She shifted under the heavy blankets, her hand rubbing across her belly.

Bare skin.

She moved her fingers around. Bare skin on her belly. On her arms. On her chest. On her legs.

Her head lifted off the pillow.

"Dom, I'm stripped to the bare under here."

He met her look straight on. "That ye are."

"No." Her head twisted to the side though she kept her gaze locked on him. "Did you?"

He shrugged. "Of course I did. The fire was barely sputtering when I got ye back here. You were soaked to the bone and I had to get the freeze of the snow off of ye."

"But—"

"But nothing. I averted my eyes." A slight grin lifted his right cheek. "My hands didn't slip…much."

"Dom—"

"I tease." He patted her ankle. "It was frightening how I managed to undress ye with the utmost propriety. Even an Almack's patroness would have approved."

She exhaled an exasperated groan and her head fell back down onto the pillow. Coming from any other man, she wouldn't believe those words. But from Domnall…she believed him. Twinkle in his blue eyes and all.

He pointed to the middle of the blankets. "Are your fingers still blue?"

She pulled her right hand free of the cover of blankets and held it in front of her. Though her muscles hurt—hell, every inch of her body ached raw—the color of her fingers seemed normal. She turned the pads of her fingers to Domnall.

He leaned over her legs, his eyes squinting at them in the light of the fire. "Aye. They look much better than they did."

She tucked her hand under the heavy wool blankets, watching him as he watched the fire and rubbed her feet.

Impossible.

She couldn't quite grasp the twist of fate that had sent him here to the earl's abbey and into her path. She'd given up years ago on ever seeing Domnall again.

Unless…unless he was here for her. And if that was the case, he'd better think again on what he thought to do here in Badenoch. She wasn't the innocent girl he'd once known.

Far from it. And she could never let him discover what she'd become.

She cleared her throat. "What are you doing here, Dom?"

"I could ask the same of you."

"I live here—well, not here at the abbey—I live at the Leviton dower house to the east of this estate. I have since Lord Leviton died."

His hands on her feet stilled. It took a long breath before he looked to her. "I've been away from Vinehill Castle—in Spain, procuring new bloodlines for the herds—so I hadn't heard the information on his passing. How long has that been?"

"He died in May."

Domnall nodded, his jaw stubbornly still, his gaze going back to the fire.

"Your turn, Dom. What are you doing here?"

His head slowly turned to her and a heavy breath lifted his massive chest. "I'm the new Earl of Kirkmere."

{ CHAPTER 4 }

She was a widow.

The viscount she'd left him for, dead.

The one woman he would have once moved mountains for. Now a widow.

He'd been attempting to wash her from his blood for the past six years.

Six long and bitterly lonely years.

She'd left him to marry the viscount. Left him without a word. Without a note. Without a chance.

Just left him. Disappeared.

Crushed his heart, leaving the shattered fragments to harden and crust with time.

And now her bare feet were on his lap. Her body sleek and naked on the settee next to him. Her long dark hair—almost black—haphazard about the pillow. Her jaw slightly agape at his admission of the earldom he'd recently inherited.

Her mouth clamped closed, the shock dissolving from her exquisite porcelain skin. "I understood Lord Kirkmere had died before Maggie and I moved up here, and they were searching for the next heir, but I never would have imagined you, of all people, to appear here, next in line."

"Neither did anyone else. Especially me. They had to search far back to find the branch that led to my"—he lifted his fingers one by one to tick off the number—"great, great, great, great-grandfather that was the youngest brother of

three boys. He died in the Dutch War—young, so it wasn't easily apparent he had a wife and child."

Karta shook her head. "Amazing. The happenstance of it."

"Aye." He met her look, noting how her amber brown eyes were the color of honey in the light of the fire. Eyes he needed to not lose himself in, for he would be forever stuck. He had to remember the cruelty she was capable of. "It is that."

"But what will Vinehill do without you? If it's been the same since I was last there, you run that estate to a fault. Lachlan must be distraught, not to mention his grandfather."

"Lach wasn't exactly happy about what it would mean for Vinehill, but he was happy for me. If anything, it is more that Lach and Eva's children didn't want me to leave. Lach understands—as does the marquess even as bitter as he was when it was first announced. Lach will manage Vinehill fine now that his grandfather has finally peeled his fingernails away from controlling everything."

"Was that even possible? The marquess was always a… force." Her toes wiggled under his palm, nudging his hands back into motion.

"Politely said." Domnall shrugged, then lifted her left foot, his thick hand slipping under her leg to massage the tight tendons. "The marquess has managed to do so, with lots of encouragement from Eva. I think the marquess is as in love with his granddaughter-in-law as Lach is. Either way, they will get on without me."

Karta nodded, her chin rubbing on the stack of blankets drowning her body. "I just know how heavily the marquess depends—depended upon you."

He nodded and his hands wrapped around her feet, drawing long strokes down against the length of them. Her feet had long since warmed, but he couldn't quite pull his fingers from her skin. Couldn't quite tuck her toes under the cover of the blankets.

For how he'd stumbled upon her in the snow—for how he'd believed not but an hour ago that he'd found her again and was about to lose her in the span of fifteen minutes—the feel of her skin, warm and pulsating with every heartbeat, grounded him to the fact that she was alive.

Next to him.

Next to him and now a widow.

A blasted widow.

Everything he could have ever wanted, if only he didn't despise her for leaving him those many years ago.

A surge of bitterness ran through his chest as the past crept forward in his mind like it always did. His look shifted to the fire. "Why did ye come to Badenoch, Karta? It's bitter cold with the wind beating through these lands and I know how you hate the cold."

"I don't hate it like I once did."

His eyebrow cocked and he glanced at her. "When did that change?"

Her dark eyelashes closed slightly, her brown eyes looking to the dark rafters in the ceiling above. "It just… did."

"I donnae hardly believe it. There was a time when ye would make me block the slightest whiff of wind from your shoulders. In the dead of summer, even."

A soft smile lifted the right side of her full lips, then quickly fell away. "Maybe it was because I've had no one to shelter me from the cold, so I had to become accustomed to it." A frown took over her bottom lip and her gaze dropped to him. "To be honest, I have been numb for the last six years and the cold here is one of the few things that makes me feel alive—makes me feel something. Even if that something is a bitter snap across my face."

Domnall's eyebrows lifted. "But it is also barren of people up here. Why not go to live in Edinburgh or, strike my words, London?"

Her frown deepened for a long moment, then she shook her head, more to herself than to him. "I was not well liked by my husband's sons from his first wife. The eldest is older than me, the other two just younger, and after my husband died, I was banished to the dower house here in Badenoch. My options have been very few."

Her words rushed far too fast from her lips. There was something she wasn't telling him.

"Why not go home to your father's estate? You'd at least be around people."

"And let him get the notion in his head that he could use me again to advance his alliances? I think not." Her voice spiked. "One marriage at the altar of his ambition was enough—not to mention the failed engagements to Jacob and then Lachlan I suffered. I've spent too many of my years tied to his machinations. I'm done with my duty to my family."

"So now ye think to hide out here in the mountains? Live out your days skulking amongst the trees and mountain heath with only your maid for company?"

She shrugged, the pile of blankets shifting upward. "Better than the alternative."

"Which is?"

Her nose wrinkled, the cut of her voice hardening. "Be pawned off onto another elderly, sallow-skinned dandy."

There it was.

The shot of deranged jealousy—of fierce protectiveness—that sliced through his belly at the slightest hint of anyone doing Karta wrong.

He'd wondered when it would appear.

It had always been visceral and it flared back to life, just as raw and angry as it always had been.

His look narrowed at her. "Did the bastard hurt ye, Karta?"

"You don't get to ask me that, Dom." Her brown eyes pierced him, boring into him as they always had. "You gave up your right to ask anything about my person long ago."

His hands tightened around her feet. "Karta—"

She jerked her toes from his grip, drawing them under the blankets and curling them up toward her body. "No. You did. You gave up everything to do with me that summer before I married the viscount."

His hands curled into fists on his lap, his jaw clenching. "I was always too old for you."

"Too old?" She shifted under the blankets, scooting away from him to sit up and set her back along the cushioned side of the settee. In a wild flurry of arms moving, she jutted out her left hand to clutch the blankets to her bare chest as she leaned forward, fire in her words. "You're ten years older than me, Dom. How is that too old? Do you even know how much older the viscount was?"

He shook his head. The last thing he wanted to do was listen to facts about her husband.

"Twenty-two years. So don't you dare speak such ridiculous drivel." Her right hand found its way free of the blankets and she pointed at him. "Excuses. Excuses as always. The thousands of reasons why we shouldn't be together. You're too old. Vinehill needed you. You had to tromp across the countryside with Lach. You came up with one excuse after another and I'd heard them all—hundreds of times. But they never dissuaded me, did they?"

A sigh escaped his lips. "No."

"But I should have listened to them. Each and every one. If I had…" Her head shook and she slumped back against the arm of the settee.

"If you had, what?"

Her lip curled as she looked at him with scorn in her brown eyes. "I would have been smart. I wouldn't have ever dared to have my heart broken by you."

His head jerked back. "I broke—what—what do you mean—I br—"

A sharp knock on the open door made both of their heads swivel toward the entrance of the room opposite the fireplace.

Stooped over with age, the Kirkmere butler stood there, looking from Domnall to Karta, his wiry grey eyebrows lifted high on his wrinkled forehead. "My lord."

It took Domnall several seconds to realize the butler was addressing him. He gave his head a slight shake. "Yes, Fredrick?"

The man lifted a wrinkled hand to his ear, cupping it as he looked at Domnall. "What was that, my lord?"

Domnall lifted his voice. "I said, yes, Frederick?"

At least the man hadn't heard him and Karta arguing. Not at Kirkmere Abbey for two hours and he already had a naked woman sitting in his drawing room. His first impression as Lord Kirkmere was not going quite as planned.

The butler nodded and what constituted a smile pulled his thin lips back. "Very good, sir. Cook has made a meal for ye and yer men and yer guest. And the men have just arrived with the maid from the dower house. They have placed the lass in one of the guest rooms above."

"The doctor?" Domnall asked.

"Has yet to arrive. Though it is farther to reach him than the dower house."

In sudden movement beside him, Karta went busy, tucking the blankets around her naked body, attempting to figure out how to gracefully stand without the cover of the blankets failing her. "Then I must go up and tend to Maggie. If she's awake, she will be most frightened. She didn't want me to leave for help."

Fredrick looked to Karta, a kind smile sending a twinkle into his greying eyes. "Mrs. Humphrey has found a

dress for ye, my lady. It is fifty years beyond fashion, but it is dry."

Karta slipped her feet to the floor in front of the fireplace, her toes avoiding Theodora's paws that were directly underneath. She quickly swept the one blanket she pulled up with her around her backside. "That would be most helpful, Fredrick. Thank you. Perhaps you could show me the way to the dress and to Maggie?"

Fredrick started shuffling in a circle to turn around before he spoke. "I would be happy to, my lady. 'Tis been a long time since a lady of yer status has graced these halls."

Karta made her way to the door, her stride stifled by the tight swathe of the blanket about her legs. She wasn't about to show more skin than necessary.

Even wrapped in an old wool blanket, she was still the epitome of exquisite grace and beauty.

Still far, far out of his reach.

Domnall heaved a breath that only made it into the top of his lungs.

Some things never changed.

CHAPTER 5

Her eyes bleary after the restless night sleeping wedged onto the short settee in the room Maggie was brought into, and then the subsequent long day tending to her, Karta walked down the main stairs of the abbey.

The doctor had arrived late last night. His prognosis—if Maggie made it through the night with her fever and closing throat, she would likely survive what he thought was scarlet fever.

So Karta had stayed in her room all night and for most of the day, checking on her maid, cooling her head, dripping water into her mouth. Everything the doctor asked of her.

Such little things that felt so insignificant in the battle against death.

Maggie was too important to her to lose. She'd been her only friend in the viscount's world, and Karta couldn't bear the thought of her maid and only friend dying.

Her hand resting on top of the newel post at the bottom of the staircase, Karta stepped down into the foyer and looked about.

Her surroundings were catching the last rays of daylight from the windows high above the front doorway, whereas everything had been dark last night as she followed Fredrick through the house to Maggie's room. The entryway of the abbey was grand, with interspersed white and dark marble lining the floors and reliefs of columns lining the

walls. Far more imposing and modern than she would have guessed from the ancient gothic stones of the abbey's exterior.

Her stomach growled and a pang of hunger twisted her belly. Where was the dining hall? She cocked her head, listening for sound.

A rumble of men's voices came from her left and she made her way down the hallway that led into that wing.

Roasted grouse filled her nostrils. The right direction.

She arrived at the entryway to the dining room just as four huge Scotsman were exiting. Jumping a step to her right, they almost ran her over in quick succession before Domnall spotted her on the side of the doorway.

"Karta."

All the men stopped in stride, turning to her.

Her hand unconsciously went to her hair, smoothing the rumpled strands from her face. She should have looked in the mirror before coming down out of Maggie's room.

Domnall tilted his head to her, motioning to his men. "Lady Leviton, ye will recall Rory."

"Of course, it is so good to see you again."

"And may I introduce Colin and Bailey." He motioned to her. "This is Lady Leviton."

Karta shook her head. "Please, it is Karta. In this odd situation I find myself in here at the abbey, it would be foolish to keep up the pretense of titles."

The three men, all of them big and thick, but not quite reaching the height of Domnall, bowed their heads to her and moved past her, disappearing down the hall. Silent Scots. The exact men Domnall would surround himself with.

Domnall didn't follow them, instead, standing at the entrance to the dining room, staring at her.

Staring so long in silence, it unnerved her.

His right forefinger tapped on the side of his leg against his black trousers. "The doctor reported to us that Maggie should recover, or was he being overly optimistic?"

"I think she will be better. Her breathing has been much more even today and she opened her eyes and almost seemed to recognize me—it's been days since that has happened."

"And you?"

"Me what?" Her eyebrows lifted.

"You were up all night tending to her, weren't ye? And then all day?"

"I—yes, for a good portion of the night and the day. How did you know?"

"You're tired—and hungry." His look ran down her body along the simple black wool dress that the housekeeper had found, and back up again. "I can see it in your face. In your eyes."

She really should have glanced in the mirror. Her hands went to her face and she rubbed her fingers under her eyes to try and perk up her skin.

He reached out and grabbed her wrist, stopping her motion. "You're as beautiful as ever. Don't worry on how you look. The true reason I know you're tired is because every time I peeked into Maggie's room last night and today, ye were at a vigil by her bedside."

"You looked in? I didn't hear you."

"You may not remember, but I can be stealthy." The corner of his lips twitched. "I didn't want to disturb. She is fortunate to have you."

"No." She shook her head. "I am the fortunate one. She has been steadfast and loyal to me throughout the years."

He turned to the side and pointed into the dining room. "There is still plenty of food. My men just wanted to eat early as they were out all day in the barns and clearing the snow and were ravenous."

Karta nodded, starting to move past him. A mistake, for he still filled most of the entryway and didn't move.

It wasn't until she was squished to the side and had to brush against him that she realized her error.

His heat.

The shock of heat from him that had always overwhelmed her and filled her body with a hunger for him that took her breath away. It encapsulated her, tightening her chest, sending her heart pounding.

For what she had admitted to him last night—how he broke her heart—she didn't want this. Didn't want his attention. Didn't want his words. Didn't want his heat.

She wanted the cold comfort of the drafts. Of the safety of the chill far, far away from him.

She could already feel her hatred for him waning and while she knew she should hold steadfast to it, stoking the coals of animosity was hard when he had just saved her life. And Maggie's life.

Her foot darted out fast and long, and she jumped past him, moving quickly into the dining room.

"Do ye mind if I join ye?"

She glanced over her shoulder at him. "It's not necessary on my account. I'm accustomed to eating in solitude."

His eyebrow cocked. "Solitude?"

She nodded, not willing to say the word again for how pathetic she realized it sounded. But she had eaten alone for years. In her father's home. In her husband's home. Long, grand tables with only one place setting.

"It is for me, truth told." He stepped back into the room with her. "I didn't eat as much as the men, for I wanted them to fill their bellies first. I stayed inside all day, shuffling through the mess of papers that was left with the estate, so I wasn't as hungry. But then Cook appeared with another full platter of roasted grouse just as they were finishing. So there is plenty for all."

Karta smiled. "Your cook is already proving her worth with the new master. Feeding hungry Scots is not an easy task."

He chuckled. "No, no, it is not. They've all more than earned their keep, the staff that is here. Especially for opening up the house as quickly as they did last night. There's nary a cold spot left in the abbey."

"Well, if you walked in as my new employer, I would jump fairly fast as well."

"Ye would?"

"You are intimidating, Dom." Her mouth quirked in a tease as she pulled a clean plate and a fork and knife from the sideboard and sat down at the table. "You do remember that, don't you?"

A scoff expelled from his lips as he copied her motions and sat down at the end of the table adjacent to her. "I forget, sometimes. Especially when I've been surrounded by the men for a long time. Or when I'm at Vinehill. Everyone there is far past being intimidated by me."

He cut into the roasted grouse and set a large chunk of the meat, dripping with steaming juices, onto her plate. "You haven't eaten anything today, so you need to catch up."

"You were watching that as well?"

His gaze caught hers, the dark blue of his eyes almost shifting into grey in the light. "I was."

Of course he was.

Domnall crushed her heart years ago, but he would still be the most attentive man she'd ever known. Infuriating.

Her attention went to the roasted potatoes and she scooped a heaping pile onto her plate. Not looking at him, she fiddled with cutting her meat. "You need to stop that, Dom."

"Stop what?"

"Paying me any mind. As soon as Maggie is well and the snow has cleared, we will be out of your way and back to the dower house. I already regret this imposition upon you."

"You regret saving Maggie's life?"

She looked up at him. "I regret that of all the places in the world, you were here last night, in the one place I never would have expected you. I regret that it didn't take me but five minutes in your presence and I was right back in the place I was six years ago. I regret that you—you make me feel alive. Whole. You always have. But I cannot go back there. Feel that. Not now." She heaved a breath. "And I regret that I've hated you for the last six years—and that the hatred that I've harbored for so long started to dissipate within moments of being next to you."

"You hated me?"

Her shoulders lifted. "I thought…I thought I did…"

She cut her own words off before she said more. Before she admitted that what she regretted most was what she'd become—and how that would keep them apart more than anything. She didn't dare to even imagine how Domnall would look at her once he knew the truth.

Her forehead dipped forward and she jabbed a piece of the grouse, stuffing it into her mouth to curb her tongue. She'd already said far too much.

His fault for always listening so attentively to her.

Another chunk of meat went into her mouth. And another. And another. She'd eaten half the food on her plate, ignoring Domnall's stare, before she reached for the glass of wine he'd poured for her when he sat down.

He hadn't even picked up his fork.

Three long sips and she went back to the food on her plate. For all that she was accustomed to eating alone, his silence unnerved her. She wasn't alone. He was sitting a breath away. The only man she'd ever loved.

But she could never allow herself to think on that again. Think of him like that again.

Her shoulders pulled back and she looked at him. "Whatever you hope to achieve with your silence, Dom, it will not work. As I said, I'm accustomed to eating alone and this is no different."

He nodded, setting his elbows on the table and clasping his large hands together under his chin. His dark blue eyes sliced into her. "Is it?"

"I can easily pretend you're not here."

"My size alone would beg to differ."

"Your size never intimidated me, Dom. It took me aback the first time I met you, yes, but after that initial moment, you have always been just you." She jabbed a potato chunk with her fork. "So yes, I can eat in silent peace and not acknowledge you exist."

He leaned forward and lifted his goblet of claret, taking a long sip, then picked up his fork. "So you remember the first time we met?"

She looked at him out of the corner of her eye. "Of course I do. It was at the stables at Vinehill. You were in a stall, pitchfork in your hand. You were showing my father and the marquess the mares that would be good options for breeding with the stud my father had just won Newmarket with. My father and the marquess had walked away and I had stopped to stroke the neck of one of the mares…"

She looked down at her plate, scanning her memory. "Rosalinda—that was the mare's name. She was a beautiful beast. The prettiest speckling. I was stroking her neck and you moved to stand next to me and you asked me what I thought of her."

She paused and the softest smile came to her face. "And I was dumbstruck."

"You were?" He set down his wine glass. "Because of my size?"

She looked at him. For all his certainty of self and purpose, Domnall had always had one insecurity—his size. His height and strength and how it would scare people. Intimidate them. It was obviously still top in his mind.

"No." Her head shook. "I was dumbstruck because you asked me the question. Do you know that aside from my grandmother, you were the first person in my life to ask me what I actually thought of something?" Her hand flipped into the air. "Beyond which clothes I should wear or how to style my hair, of course."

"Ye were dumbstruck?" He chuckled. "I was dumbstruck. I was lucky I got any words out at all. I do recall I just wanted to hear your voice. Ye could have talked about butterflies for all I cared. I just needed to hear your voice in that moment. Change the enigma of ye into a real person. And then the oddest thing happened."

Her eyebrows quirked. "What?"

"Ye were intelligent. Ye went down a list of the multitudes of considerations for the breeding of each of the mares I had shown your father and the marquess—and not only the attributes that had been discussed, but how those attributes played with the factors I hadn't considered—the horses' reactions when approached by a male. Their pride. Their personalities. Not just the length of their stride or the breadth of their thighs."

Without taking a bite of grouse, he set his fork down and picked up his glass again, tilting it to her before taking a sip. "And you were right on every accord. Ye designed some of the best matches ever made from the Vinehill stables that day."

"Do not short yourself, Dom. You always do that." She pointed at him with the tines of her fork. "We designed the matches. The both of us. I talked, but you not only asked me questions—you actually listened to my answers. Countered my points. And we were both better for it."

She exhaled a breath, her hand gripping her fork dropping to the table as her look went to her plate. Her voice faltered. "We always were." Her gaze lifted to him. "How did we lose that?"

A flash of anger flickered across his face. Come and gone so quickly she wasn't even sure she saw it. Domnall had always been able to do that. Hide each and every emotion he had from her.

Except for how he had once wanted her. That he hadn't been able to hide.

He wanted her. His body, the heat in his dark blue eyes whenever they had been alone in a corridor or in the stables.

But she hadn't been enough for him.

The humiliation of that fact still burned a hole in her gut. Unforgotten. She wasn't enough. She'd never been what her father wanted her to be. Domnall was just the next in line.

She stared at her half-eaten food, not able to lift her fork to it. Her appetite had vanished.

Domnall cleared his throat, his voice rough. "You're beautiful, Karta—beyond compare. And then I learned ye were smart. That ye took in all that was around you, but ye were never allowed to speak. From the very first, I knew I never had a chance with you. Even though I lied to myself for years on the matter. Ye were destined to marry Jacob. He was heir to Vinehill. After he died, there was one minute where I had hope, but then the marquess deemed you were to marry Lachlan."

He shook his head. "One brother to another. And I always knew, deep down, you were made for grand estates and diamonds and London and balls and silk dresses. And I couldn't give ye any of that."

Her fork slammed down onto her plate, her ire spiking. She wasn't about to let him hide behind that excuse. Not now. Not after all these years. "And that is exactly why you were my match. You didn't care about any of those things. You couldn't give me all of that—only you. Only yourself. That was all you could give me and all I ever wanted. The biggest, strongest man in Scotland. A man who saw beneath what my father created in me—the gilded lady that he demanded me to be. You saw everything beneath that. But then I wasn't enough for you."

"What in the devil's name do you mean, Karta?" He set his goblet down on the table, his own voice rising against hers. "Ye said that last night—I broke your heart. When? When could I have possibly done that?"

Her lip curled, her head shaking, and she shoved back in her chair, jumping to her feet as she leaned over the table to him. Even standing she barely had an inch on his height. "Don't even try that. You didn't come, Dom. I waited and you didn't come."

"Come to what?"

"The blasted midsummer ball." Her palm slammed onto the table. "You told me you were coming, but you didn't. So that was it. That was the end of our time."

His brow furrowed. "What? What madness are ye speaking? You left me because of a damned ball?"

"Not because of a damned ball." She shoved off from the table, her hand flying in the air. "There was no more time. I made a deal with my father—I risked everything—everything on you. If you came for me by the midsummer ball, he would consider you. Consider letting me marry you. You don't know what it took to convince him of that. But the only way he agreed to it was if you didn't come by the ball…if you didn't, I was to marry the viscount. You had months, Dom. Months. And you swore you were coming. You swore it again and again. But you didn't show, Dom."

Her fingers curled into a fist and she knocked it onto the table, the sound a dull thud. "You didn't show. So I stood by my word. I left the next morning for the Leviton estate."

He pushed back his own chair, standing, towering over her. "I showed up the next day after that ball, Karta. The next day. I bloody well told ye I was coming for you, and I did."

Her arms clasped over her chest, her look flinging daggers up at him. "Yes, well, you were obviously delayed."

"You're telling me I was hours late? I missed ye by a few blasted hours?"

Her shoulders lifted and she took a step toward him, her voice lifting into a growl. "I don't know—I don't know when you showed up. No one ever said anything about it and it didn't matter. I was gone. Done with you. I made the deal with my father and I was bound to it."

"Ye should have damn well told me you made a blasted deal with your father." His words slowed, his head shaking. "Ye set everything upon that moment and ye didn't even tell me."

"If I was important enough—you would have come." Her palm slapped onto her chest, her neck craning to look up at him. "I trusted you to come because you said you would. Do you know I stood there that entire night, refusing to dance, my eyes on the entrance? I was in the exact spot where I thought I would be easy to find, in front of the pillars just to the left of the French doors leading to the gardens. And I had the vision of you coming through the double doors, filling the width of them, your blue eyes searching all the corners of the room until you found me. And then you would spot me and cut across the dance floor and pull me into your arms in front of everyone. Marking me as yours in front of my father, in front of everyone. And life would be right—our life, together."

The rage in her voice petered and she had to swallow a shaking breath. "I waited until the ballroom was empty and they snuffed the candles, Dom. I waited alone in the dark. And not once in those moments did I doubt you would show. I knew you were coming. But then the morning rays started streaming in. And my father appeared." Her eyes closed, her head shaking. "If only you would have shown like you promised you would, Dom. But you didn't."

Her lips pulled inward, her gaze skewering him. "You made that choice—I wasn't important enough."

{ CHAPTER 6 }

"Not important enough?" He looked down at her, at the fury lining her brown eyes, at her strained lips.

That she could even think such a blasphemy spiked the blood in his veins, his chest twisting at the injustice of it.

That he'd been vilified for being late to a damned ball. That she'd ever believed she wasn't important enough.

And then he saw it. The quiver in her irises. The pain. The pain in her brown eyes that she was trying to cover up with indignation.

Pain at something he'd done.

His breath stilled.

He had promised her he would come to the ball, and he didn't.

He'd failed her.

He'd failed himself.

And he hadn't even known it until that very moment.

He'd always blamed her for leaving him. Leaving without a word. Leaving everything they'd dreamed about being together.

She had been the one that left him.

Except she hadn't.

He hadn't shown at the ball. Hadn't shown until the day after.

And the pain of that moment—of that destruction he'd caused in her heart—still vibrated six years later in her amber brown eyes.

Pain he needed to make disappear.

Pain he had no words to lessen.

He stepped toward her, closing the space between them, his body brushing against her arms clamped in front of her.

His hands clasped onto her face and he leaned down, his lips meeting hers in a storm. She stilled for a second, her body going rigid, almost as though she was to fight it.

But then her lips parted to him.

Parted to him, but angry. Angry that he was here. Angry at what they had lost. Angry that she still could not deny him—deny how their bodies needed each other. He absorbed all of that in the kiss as she met him with fire in every breath, every swipe of his tongue against her lips.

She didn't back away. She met him move for move like she always had.

He pulled slightly up, his voice raw. "Whatever you thought, Karta, you have it wrong. You were always the one—the only—important thing."

She flinched, her voice cracking. "Then where were you?"

"I don't even know." He shook his head, his look going to the ceiling. "Out for the marquess, checking on the new flocks, if I recall. But I do remember I was muddy and exhausted and I had to clean myself before appearing at your father's home and I thought you would understand."

"So it was just another time you chose the almighty Vinehill estate over me."

His look dropped to her, skewering her. "Ye ken that's not true. That it was never true."

"Wasn't it? Because your bloody loyalty to them was all I ever heard about from you. Every excuse I ever heard from your lips was lined with the needs of Vinehill."

Her arms unthreaded from her chest. "We couldn't be together because I was betrothed to Vinehill men—first Jacob, then Lachlan. We couldn't be together because the marquess needed you to scour the estate for his blasted sheep. We couldn't be together because Lachlan needed you to tramp about the countryside with him, scouting roadways. We couldn't be together because you had to go out to collect the rents. We couldn't be together because you couldn't leave the family in crisis after the fire that took Jacob. We couldn't be together for hundreds of reasons and every single one of them had to do with Vinehill."

His lips pulled inward, this battle that he'd fought with her a thousand times rearing up from deep in the past. "Ye know why I'm loyal to them. Ye cannot ask me to be otherwise."

"I can't?" She grabbed his upper arm, the touch sending fire into his veins.

The first time she'd voluntarily reached out and touched him since he'd found her in the snow.

Her look pinned him. "I know you were an orphan. I know they took you in. I know that they built you up to be all that you are. I know that they are your family. But what about me, Dom?"

His stare shifted from her, fixating on the silver platters of food on the sideboard.

"Look me in the eye, Dom." Her fingers dug into the muscles in his upper arm.

His jaw flexing, his gaze dropped to her.

"What about me? What about living for yourself? For me? That was what we were going to do. Us, together, a farm, a flock of sheep—I didn't care. All I wanted was you. And you know the marquess would have given you whatever you asked for. He's a wicked old devil, but he rewards those that are loyal—and there have been none more loyal than you. He regards you as one of his grandsons."

Everything she said he knew to be true. And that grated on him all the more. "I had planned to do all of that, Karta. But I didn't know I was on a blasted time limit."

"You didn't know?" She shook his arm. "No, don't try that, Dom. I told you—I told you how important it was for you to be at that ball. I told you our life together depended upon it."

"Yes, but you'd said that before, again and again—our future depended on me being somewhere—at a ball, at the horse racing your father sponsors, at the Vinehill dinners. Our future always depended on those things—but all those I missed, it was because I was working on our future, working on how I would exit Vinehill."

Her body stilled, her hand dropping from his arm. "Yes, well, you ran out of time."

She took a step backward—away—and her hip bumped into the chair.

"Don't move away from me, not now." The words came out in a low roar.

"Why not now, Dom?"

"Not when you are in front of me for the first time in six years and I realize exactly how I failed ye. Not when there is the slightest possibility that I can right whatever wrongs there were of the past. Not when I want ye more than I ever have. Not when this unlikely gift of the two of us together again—trapped, with nothing but time— appeared out of nowhere just before Christmas."

He stepped closer, staring down at her, waiting. Waiting for the slightest motion, the slightest indication that all was not lost between them.

Her dark lashes fell closed. Her chest rising in one breath. Two. Three.

Her full lips parted. "It can't be the same, Dom."

He stared at her closed eyes. She was teetering. Opening up her heart to the possibility.

His words rumbled low from his chest. "I don't want it the same. I want you. However you come to me now, I take ye."

Her brown eyes, warm with streaks of honey gold, opened to him. Uncertainty, but it was there in her look. The possibility.

His mouth descended on hers, taking her into a kiss.

He felt it instantly, the quiver that ran through her, that sent her body pressing into his. He parted his lips, edging hers open. No resistance. Plunging. Descending into the depths of the kiss, the draw of how their bodies had always needed to be touching.

His tongue slipped out and tasted the sweetness of her mouth. Sweetness and heat. Matching him with every swipe of his tongue, every shift of his lips.

The slightest mewl bubbled in her throat and her hand lifted, her fingers burying into the back of his hair. Holding him close, not letting him leave her for even a breath.

His hand on the small of her back trailed upward along her side, his thumb curving under the swell of her breasts. She didn't jerk away, only leaned into his touch. His fingers went up, rubbing across her nipple, dipping beneath the lace that lined the bodice of her dress. Down. Further. Deeper until he reached the dimpled skin of her nipple. He rolled the bud in his fingers and she gasped, her head slipping backward as a low hum vibrated in her throat.

Her neck bared to him, he descended, his lips hungry on her skin, trailing downward. He was at her nipple before the thought of control entered into his head. He set his lips to it, his tongue swirling over the nubbin, sparking it to strain deeper into his mouth as her hips pressed into him, swaying against his already throbbing cock.

He took the nubbin between his teeth and it sent a gasp of pleasure from her lips. His gaze lifted upward for one moment to look at her, to watch the pleasure flash across her exquisite features.

Heaven. Heaven in front of him.

His head dipped and he took another swipe of his tongue across her nipple. "Hell, Karta, you taste like summer."

Words that broke the spell she was under.

She jerked away from him, her fingers rubbing her swollen lips. Her left hand tugged the bodice of her dress up over her nipple as her words came out breathless. "I don't know if I can do this, Dom."

"Why not?"

"You're breaking me and I cannot be broken again."

"I'm not going to break you, Karta."

Her hands went up between them, pressing against his chest. "I'm not who I once was. I haven't been that woman you knew for a long time. Those years with the viscount… they changed me."

His look narrowed at her. "Don't tell me you're still loyal to the man." A spike of jealousy sent his gut churning. "I don't know anything of the viscount, but I know he couldn't touch ye like I touch you." He pushed forward into her hands on his chest and kissed her so hard there would be no room in her mind for anyone but him.

He broke contact, yet his lips stayed a hair away, brushing hers. "Kiss ye like I kiss you."

Her head craned back, her eyes wide. "No, Dom—he was different—different than you. He didn't touch me like you do."

He blinked hard. And again. She was still talking about the bastard.

The cold clamp of jealousy slithered around his chest. "So ye thought of me when you were under him?"

She jerked back and slapped him, the sting barely registering through the fury that had gripped him at the thought of her under that decrepit old viscount.

"No." She fumbled to the side, scrambling away from the table and him, her voice in a screeching whisper. "Leonard was frail and he was nothing like you, Dom. Nothing. "

Domnall stepped away from her, his head shaking as he tried to squelch the jealous rage in his chest. "I apologize. That was out of line."

"It sure as hell was." She yanked her bodice fully into place and backed away from him. "Make no mistake. The day I left my father's home was the day I stopped thinking of you."

His hands curled into fists at his sides and his voice went bitterly hard. "I don't believe you, Karta."

She stalked to the door, her fingers waving in the air, dismissing him. "Believe what you must. Whatever sets your head on a pillow and lets you sleep. It's not my concern and it never should have been."

{ CHAPTER 7 }

He was getting too close.

A day in the same house with the obstinate man and he was already too close to finding his way in, to finding out what she'd become.

She couldn't have that.

It was clear he didn't know what had happened to her or he never would have approached her—sat down with her.

Kissed her.

And he could never know. Not for the way his face would crumple when he learned the truth. Not for how he would look at her with disgust once he knew.

Leaving Kirkmere Abbey had been the best choice. Her only choice after that scene in the dining hall. His mouth on hers. His strength around her.

Dangerous. All of it dangerous to her very sanity.

Better to distance herself from him now—this very eve—before everything became so complicated there was no way to untangle her heart from him again.

Karta lifted her hand, rubbing the tip of her cold nose with her leather riding glove. It scratched rough against her skin, the leather still not worn soft again after being soaked by the snow when she had walked to the abbey.

From high on the horse she had borrowed from the Kirkmere stables, Karta's gaze fell to the dark of the trees that lined the side of the Leviton dower house. The moon

reflected bright off the white landscape and sent long black shadows of tree branches to snake along the smooth white snow.

Shadows that taunted her, aching to pull her back into the exile of the Leviton dower house.

Her look moved upward, setting straight ahead to the stable behind the dower house. It had been right to leave the abbey. The doctor had agreed to stay with Maggie until she was well. With luck, Maggie would rejoin her at the dower house in a few days. And then Karta could attempt to pretend the last day and a half had never happened.

She nodded to herself. She would be fine on her own for a few days. It would give her silent time when she could work on purging from her mind the fact that Domnall was now living directly across the glen from her.

The horse nickered, snorting as it stepped through the deep snow up the short hill to the stable.

Her eyes scanned the front of the barn as they approached it. Damn. The snow was still drifted in front of the doors leading into the stable. Even higher than before.

Karta halted the horse, staring for a long moment at the heavy black iron latch holding the doors closed. She exhaled a long sigh, then leaned forward, patting the mare on the side of her neck. "Don't worry, girl. I'll get you into the warmth."

She nudged the horse forward another four steps and then dismounted, dropping with a thud into a drift of snow.

Her fingers were already cold, but there was nothing for it. She couldn't leave the magnificent beast standing in the freezing cold, nor could she let her own horses go any longer without food and water.

She trudged through the snow, the top layer of it now crusted over to a thin sheet of ice that shattered apart against her knees with every step as she pushed against the drifts.

She stopped before the door on the right, kicking at the drift in front of it with her boot, and then she unhinged the latch and grabbed the black handle, pulling as hard as she could.

The door only opened a hand's width.

She looked over her shoulder at the horse. "No, you're a bit bigger than that, aren't you?"

She swiped the bank of snow a few more times with her feet. It didn't take long to realize she was getting nowhere, and she bent over, scooping clumps of snow about her legs and tossing them behind her.

The snow now cleared in a small triangle about her boots, she yanked on the door again. It moved. Slightly.

She exhaled out a deep breath of air, the puff freezing into moon-lit crystals before her face. The whole damn area in front of the door would have to be cleared.

Stifling a sigh, she dropped to her knees, sweeping her arms across the snow in long strokes, pushing it away from the door.

Fifteen minutes of shoving snow on her hands and knees and she was panting with sweat on her brow. She looked up from the spot she was in. Only a quarter of the way to the hinges of the door.

Her arms screaming with the effort, she tucked her chin into her chest and dug her knees into the cold ground to keep moving, keep clearing.

How was there this much snow in the world?

Her focus stayed on the white mounds of freezing torture until she heard a faint bark. Or what she thought was a bark. It could have been an angry squirrel, irate that all its nuts were lost under the snow.

Another bark, closer, louder, and her horse whinnied, stepping in place, anxious to be out of the cold.

Karta's head popped up from below the bank of snow and she searched the white landscape, the moon sending it into an eerie glow. A horse and man appeared beside the main house with a deerhound bounding in front of it, barking, leaping in and out of the snow.

A dog she knew.

A man she knew.

She stayed on her knees, watching him approach, her chest lifting high with each heaving breath she took into her lungs.

By the time his horse sidled up to hers, she'd caught her breath from the exertion of pushing the snow, though it still quivered in her chest, ready to be taken away at any moment.

Domnall always did that to her—quickened her breath, threatened to steal it. Some things never changed, no matter how she pretended that they had.

"Ye bloody well left, Karta." The thunder in his voice as he halted his horse told her everything she needed to know about his opinion on the matter.

Her gloved hands thudded onto the front of her thighs. She looked up at him as a gust of wind hit her cheek and she cringed against it. "I did."

Shaking his head, grumbling, he swung his leg over his horse and dismounted, his heavy boots landing on the ground and sending vibrations under her knees.

He moved to tower over her, blocking the light of the moon and sending her into a deep shadow.

"Ye left to roll about in the freezing snow?"

Her look went to the stars in the clear sky. "I still cannot get the door open enough to get the mare in. I was digging the area free."

"Ye shouldn't be out here, Karta—you almost froze to death once in the past day, let's not make it twice."

"But I need to get the mare in."

He looked to his left at the horses. His stare dropped back down to her. "Or you can come back to the abbey."

Her throat collapsed on her and she shook her head. "I cannot."

From what she could see in the deep shadow shrouding his face, his bottom lip jutted up as a growl bubbled from his chest.

He turned from her, stomping through the snow to the side of the stable, and he disappeared around the corner of the field stone building. She could hear him tromping about, muttering nonsensical words to himself.

He reappeared, a long plank of wood in his hands. Moving to her side, he towered over her again. "Then get yourself up and out of the blasted snow."

"I can do this, Dom. I don't need your help." She bent down, swiping at the snow, her look down and avoiding him. "I didn't ask you to come after me."

He grabbed her wrist on mid swipe, his fingers digging into her flesh through the leather of her gloves. "No. But I'm here and I'm not going to watch ye dig out the snow. Nor let your damnable pride set ye into freezing to death." He shook his head. "Hell, Karta, you're already shaking with the cold."

He released her wrist and wedged the wood into the drift next to him. His hand dove into his greatcoat, pulling free a silver flask he thrust to her. "Drink this. It'll warm you faster than anything else. And move away from there." He pointed to the spot she was working on clearing.

She drew a deep breath, then looked about the snow still piled all around her, drifted higher than her head in some spots.

For how much she wanted to argue it out with him, she was cold.

And tired.

And her bothersome pride usually did get her into trouble.

She grabbed the flask from him and rocked back onto her heels, then stood, stepping back into the small area she'd managed to clear. Opening the cap of the flask, she took a sip as she watched him start to shovel the snow aside with the plank of wood. The sting of the whisky curled her tongue, burning down her throat.

But the burn was good. Strong against the chill her body was quickly slipping into now that she had stopped moving.

Domnall dug back heavy scoops of snow, moving them from the side of the barn outward. Swearing at her the entire time under his breath.

In five minutes, he'd cleared more than she had been able to do in a half hour with her hands.

"Bloody stubborn lass." He flipped a mound of snow into the air, the flakes separating and creating a glowing white curtain in the moonlight. "Ye always were too headstrong for your own good."

She stared at the width of him, the ease with which he plowed through the bank of snow. "And you were always too strong for your own good." She took another sip of the whisky.

He stopped, standing upright and turning around to her, his brow furrowed. "What?"

Her fingertips went over her mouth. "Did I say that out loud?"

"Aye. Ye did."

Her lips pulled inward for a long breath.

"What did ye mean, Karta?"

"I meant…" A long exhale escaped her chest. "I meant everyone always wanted to use you because of it—you were wanted for your brawn—the strongest man around. That's why you're too strong for your own good. Those at Vinehill never wanted you for your mind. For your kindness. For your astute observations. For the person you truly are." She paused, tipping the flask up to her mouth for a healthy

swallow. "That's what I always wanted—you. Not for what you could do with your muscles, but for who you are. Your soul."

His eyes narrowed at her, his fingers tightening around the edge of the board. "I knew that, Karta. I did."

"Did you?" She shrugged, looking to her left at the horses waiting impatiently in the snow. "For if you had, you would have shown at the ball."

He spun from her, thrusting the board deep into the drift of snow before him and continuing to dig in silence. The set of his shoulders was rigid—taut and angry.

She took another swallow of the whisky as she watched his jerking movements.

It wasn't fair and she knew it.

She couldn't keep blaming him for how they were parted. He hadn't known what was at stake by not showing at the ball. But the fact that he didn't arrive in time still burned bitter deep in her belly. The humiliation of it. The loss of everything she'd truly thought she could have. If he had loved her—wanted her enough—he would have shown. If she'd been the most important thing to him, he would have upheld his promise to be at the ball on time.

But she wasn't.

They hadn't been anything that she thought they were. And that stung most of all.

Domnall got to the last corner of the drift by the barn, clearing it quickly. Sticking the board into the tall mound of snow he'd just shifted, he went to the door of the barn and pulled it open. The four horses inside whinnied at the gust of air going into the stable.

Karta stepped to her horse and grabbed the mare's reins, leading her into the stable. Domnall brushed past her as she went in, then went to retrieve his horse and followed her.

So he was staying.

She eyed him over her shoulder as she led the mare into an open stall and started to work free the girth of the sidesaddle. He'd led his horse into the empty stall next to her and busied himself with removing his saddle.

How long did he think to stay here?

Five minutes? An hour?

And why?

Hell.

She shook her head. She knew exactly why. That was the trouble.

Her look went forward and she concentrated on the leather of the strap she was attempting to free. Her fingers were still shaking from the cold. The whisky had warmed her belly but not her limbs.

His feet shuffled across the floor, stopping at the entrance to her stall. "Why is it ye cannot come back to the abbey, Karta?" His words, soft and raw, drifted across the stale air to her.

She didn't turn to look at him, instead setting her focus on her trembling fingers on the leather strap and wishing them still.

Her shoulders lifted in a shrug, her gaze locked on her hands. "I don't have the answer for that. Not now. You appeared in that field last night—oddly and magically so, and it wasn't something I was expecting. I was expecting

death to come for me. Not you. You were not something I ever could have dreamed. So I don't yet know what to think on it."

Her head lifted and she looked at him over her shoulder. "But I cannot be near you—not without you drawing me into something I cannot control."

"Why do ye want to control it?" The heat in his dark blue eyes seared her. "We never could fight what was between us. And now ye are free. I am free. So why is that something to run away from?"

She spun on her heel to face him, her fingers lifting to point at his face. "Because of this. Because of how you look at me. How your voice drops into a low rumble. When you stare at me like that, when you talk to me like that, I am the exact same girl I was years ago when I would get lost in everything about you. But I'm not that same girl anymore. I can't be. So this thing between us—it has to be controlled. You look at me as you do and I have to hold stalwart against it. I once risked everything for that look of yours, and I paid dearly for that gamble."

For a long moment his stare pierced her, more heated than a breath ago. Then he smiled, forced, covering whatever it was he truly wanted to say. "So let us take care of the horses and then go into the dower house, warm up, and prove how very controlled we can be."

Karta blinked hard, her head snapping back.

Spoken by the very devil himself.

Controlled? The two of them?

Her chest tightened.

There were secrets she needed to keep and if she didn't gain some semblance of control, she would break.

Something she was determined not to do.

{ CHAPTER 8 }

"It's still chilly in here."

"It's a large room to heat." Resting on his heels as
he jabbed at the coals at the base of the fire he'd started,
Domnall lifted himself to standing and leaned the fire poker
against the grey marble that lined the hearth. Theodora
nudged his leg from where she sat next to him and with one
scruff behind Theodora's left ear, he turned to Karta. Where
she'd disappeared to for the last twenty minutes, he didn't
know.

She'd stopped just inside the doorway to the drawing
room. She hadn't yet removed her cloak, the dark folds of
it still swallowing her whole. He'd removed his great coat
when he'd come in, but for how warm he usually was, even
he could feel the snap of cold hanging in the air of the
drawing room. "Should I go up and start the fire in your
bedroom?"

"No, this room will be fine. The settee is comfortable
enough to sleep upon." She lifted her hands from the drape
of the cloak and held up a thick-cut crystal decanter full of
amber liquid and two glasses that clinked together. "I tried
several times to light the fire in the kitchens to warm up
water for tea, but my fingers wouldn't cooperate. So this will
have to do."

He resisted lifting an eyebrow. His flask had been
noticeably lighter when she'd handed it back to him outside.
But if a touch more spirits would take the cold blue from

her lips and quiver from her fingers, he wasn't about to argue with the method.

Three long strides and he was across the drawing room to her. "It's what I would prefer, as it is." He needed something to steady his hands against touching her—he'd not but minutes ago promised her control inside the house, so now he had to deliver.

He took the glasses from her grip and set them down on the side table next to the settee he'd shifted into place in front of the fire.

She moved next to him, filling both tumblers half full with the brandy from the decanter.

She handed him one, then motioned to the fire. "Come, sit?"

His brow furrowed. "You are encouraging us to be in the same room, to sit on the same cushion?"

"I am. Just being apart from you for a few minutes has given me time to breathe. Time to regain my equilibrium." Her hand wrapped around her glass. "And now that I have my senses back about me, I realize I'm being rude if I demand that you return to the abbey post-haste. For I am grateful that you appeared when you did. I do not have quite the same capability that you do for clearing that snow." She lifted her glass to him. "And I believe that the mare I borrowed is the most thankful of all."

The side of his mouth quirked upward. "I didn't imagine you would be thanking me for following you. You are thanking me, are you not?"

She nodded, a wry smile crossing her lips as she moved to sit on the settee. "Yes, I am. And why would I not?"

"You're stubborn."

A guffaw left her mouth. "Yes, but I'm also older and wiser than I once was and my fingers were about to crack off of my hands out there, so I'm not so stubborn I cannot thank you."

He couldn't hide a smile as he went to the fire. He turned the top log, scruffed Theodora's head as she splayed onto her belly close to the fire, and then moved to sit on the opposite end of the settee.

Taking a sip of the brandy, he studied her profile. She was as beautiful as the day he had first seen her—more so, even, as she had the look of the world about her. The confidence that only times of sorrow can bring a person— confidence in the quiet acceptance that the world is not all sunshine and rainbows. Her gaze was decidedly set forward, her fingertips tapping on the glass.

"Ye know it's Christmas the day after tomorrow," he said.

She glanced at him, then quickly shifted her stare back to the fire as a shiver shook her body. "Yes. And I thought to be alone. Well, alone with Maggie."

"Why alone? You did not think to travel back to your father's home?"

She shook her head. "No. Certainly not back to father. Christmastide hasn't been happy there since my grandmother died. And the sadness of that is most poignant there."

"Your grandmother—you never truly told me about her, just that she raised ye after your mother died in childbirth."

Her right cheek lifted in a mischievous smile. "Well, there was never any time for long conversations between us when we were alone together. The short walks. The moments stolen in the stables." She took a sip of her brandy, her brown eyes warm honey as she looked at him. "It was hard to think of much else besides wanting to touch you."

He chuckled, a grin taking over his face. "There was that."

"There was." She nodded.

"Take off that blasted cloak you're hiding in and come here."

"Why?" Her countenance went from gaiety to trapped rabbit.

"You're still shivering. Your cloak is clearly damp and is just keeping the chill to your body instead of warming ye. I, on the other hand, am very toasty."

She gave him an incredulous look, her fingers flipping between them. "You realize this will do nothing to improve the control we lack over what happens between us when we are too close."

"Or it will prove how much restraint we can have."

Her eyebrows cocked.

"I wouldn't take advantage of a shivering cold lass, Karta. Ye know that."

Her head tilted to the side and she sighed. "I do." She handed him her glass. "Fine."

She unhooked the clasp on the front of her wool cloak and peeled it away from her body, then draped it off the side arm of the settee. Hesitating for a moment, a shiver racked through her body. It set her into motion and she scooted along the rose damask upholstery until she was next to him.

Close, but only barely touching him. The edge of her thigh was the one point on her body that slightly grazed him.

She wasn't going to get warm like that.

He handed her glass back to her and wrapped his left arm around her shoulders.

A second of stiff resistance and then she slightly relaxed, letting him tug her tight along his torso. She pulled her feet up from the floor, quickly untying her boots with her free hand and then slipping them and her stockings off. She tucked her toes under her skirts along the back of the settee.

Still slightly stiff, she snuggled into his chest, the cold blanket of her taking over his warmth. She was far colder than he'd guessed. He should have demanded this earlier.

Just as he settled his arm down along her side, she flattened her body as much as she could against his mass, expanding the amount of warmth she could suck from him.

Absurd extraordinary pride flooded him. For all he could never give her, he could give her this. Heat.

Her shivers ceasing, her body went limp along him.

"You were talking of your grandmother—tell me more of her."

Though her arms were folded and curled tight to her chest, she managed to lift her glass that was wedged between them and take a sip of the brandy. She had to clear her throat before talking. "She died...maybe ten years before I met you. She was everything to me. It was the two of us, always together. Women of grand purpose, she would call us—so silly to the little girl I was. But she was so intelligent."

A soft smile came to her lips. "And she created these marvelous marzipan candies that were shaped like tiny animals at Christmastide every year. Rabbits, and dogs, and cats, and birds. And then she would hide them throughout the estate. Half of them—the best ones—she would tie strings to that weaved throughout the rooms, and I would follow the strings to find them. It would take days to discover them all and father hated the mess of it."

Her head shook as her eyes glazed over. "But grandmother, she loved it. Her face when I found one—she was almost in tears she was so happy, because I was so happy—like it hurt her physically to see me laughing and so joyous. I loved each and every one of those candies, those odd little marzipan masterpieces. They were perfect times—those days on Christmas."

"But then she passed?"

Karta nodded, her head rubbing against his chest. "She did, quietly in her sleep. It wasn't dramatic. She just slipped away. And with it, my whole world just slipped away." She paused, taking another sip of her brandy. "And then it was just father and I. And you know how he is."

Domnall stared down at her dark brown hair, almost black, were it not for the strands that caught amber streaks in the light of the fire.

He did know.

He knew too intimately what a bastard her father could be. How he'd told Domnall not to touch his daughter.

How he'd sworne he would tear Domnall down if he kept up his inane pursuit of Karta. How he'd threatened to have Domnall removed from Scotland for good.

But Domnall had never listened to him.

Maybe he should have.

Falling in love with Karta had brought him nothing but grief—not that he could have resisted the indomitable draw between the two of them.

"Your father." Domnall jerked upright away from the cushions, the shout echoing about the room as brandy splashed wide from both of their glasses.

"What?" Karta twisted upright, flicking off splatters of brandy from her dark blue skirt. "What about my father?"

Domnall stared at the fire, working through it in his brain for several seconds—making sure he remembered the whole of it correctly.

He had it right.

His gaze lifted to Karta, his words slow, low. "It wasn't an errand on the lands I was doing for the marquess—it was, but it wasn't."

Wrinkles creased her brow. "What are you talking about, Dom?"

"I'm talking about the night of the ball. Where I was."

Her voice went cold. "And just where were you?"

"It was your father—how did I never put it together? Of course, I never knew why you left me. But your bloody father planned the whole blasted thing—he was the one that delayed me from the ball."

He shook his head, his lip curling into a sneer. "He was the one that sent word to the marquess that one of the

Vinehill's sheep flocks on the southern border by his land had been driven into a gully that they couldn't get out of. They needed the strongest men to get them out. And of course that meant me."

Her head snapped back, her eyes wide. "No...no...he couldn't have."

"He did. He knew exactly what he was putting into motion."

Her body deflated, collapsing back against the settee, her hands in her lap, clutching the tumbler in her hand. "No...but we made a deal, father and I."

"You of all people know what sort of a man your father is, Karta. You honored the deal your way—with integrity. He honored it in his way—with manipulation."

"But—"

"Has your father ever made a deal where he didn't get exactly what he wanted?"

She stared at him, disgust quickly taking over the confusion in her brown eyes. With an exhale, she shook her head.

"Exactly."

Her eyes closed to him, her unsteady breath lifting her chest. A blow to her just the same as it was to him—probably worse, because there would always be a part of Karta that wanted to believe in her father, wanted to believe that there was good in him.

Good that Domnall had never seen in the man. He'd always guarded his tongue when it came to her father. Maybe he shouldn't have.

Her eyes flew open. "But you."

"Me what?" he asked, his voice wary.

"No matter what my father machinated. It was your choice. You didn't need to go. You didn't need to help. The marquess would have just sent other men in your stead. It still comes down to the fact that you didn't appear." Her voice cracked, her lips pulling inward. "Why didn't you come for me, Dom?"

Hell.

Why didn't he come for her?

He hadn't known what was at stake, yes.

But that was no excuse.

He'd told her he'd be there, and he wasn't. His work at Vinehill had been too important. Too important to set aside for the woman he loved. A choice that had seemed so inconsequential at the time had steered their lives so vastly apart.

And he'd been paying for that decision ever since. For there was no explanation. Not a good enough one.

He turned fully to her, bearing the weight of the tormented look on her face. How his actions so long ago wounded her so deeply.

He set his gaze directly on hers. "I don't know that I even chose what my life was long ago—I just lived it. I owed Vinehill—the marquess—everything. Everything I had, everything I was. It was because of him. I was an orphan. He took me into his home. Raised me as one of his own. So why would I ever question what was asked of me?"

Her lips pursed, but she didn't argue. She was listening.

He would take it.

"All I can tell you, Karta, is that I would change the past if I could. It was never because I didn't love you. I would have moved mountains for you. I still would."

He paused, shaking his head. "But I can't change the past. I know that." He reached out, setting his hand gently on her knee. "I can only speak to now. To this moment. And now—now I am beholden to no one. Not the marquess. Not Vinehill. I'm only beholden to that pile of stones across the glen that I inherited."

Her look had dropped to his hand on her knee.

He wasn't sure if she was about to flick it off of its perch or grab it.

A long moment passed.

She grabbed it.

"It's not exactly a pile of stones, Dom." Her brown eyes lifted, meeting his gaze. "The structure is actually quite beautiful—I've always admired it."

A change in subject.

It wasn't forgiveness, but it wasn't continued vilification. Progress.

With a shrug, his hand flipped over under her fingers, setting his palm flat against hers. "The abbey is crumbling in areas. It's going to take much work to right it. To right the estate after the neglect it has suffered the last several years."

"I didn't know the last Lord Kirkmere had neglected it so. Though I've heard very little gossip about the area. The staff here is tight-lipped about everything around me. They regard me as a suspicious lowlander." She shivered. "Maggie at least has traces of her Highland accent, so she has gotten on well enough with them."

He slipped his hand out from under hers and set his arm around her shoulders, tugging her back onto him. She didn't fight him, flattening her cold body against his chest once more.

"The last Kirkmere was quite addled at the end, from what I've been told. He apparently became quite confused about what age he was living in—the poor old chap thought the war in America had just begun. Just before the war ended, his only son was drunk in Stirling when he was pressed onto a warship and then died before it even reached America. So I guess that's the time he wanted to live in— when his son was still alive."

Her head shook. "Tragic. I can imagine going back in time like that in the end of life—especially to happier times."

He looked down at the top of her head. "When would you live?"

She angled her face to look up at him, a grin playing about her lips. "I think I'll refuse to answer that for fear the control we are exhibiting would be ruined."

She took the last sip of her brandy, then tucked the back of her fingers holding the glass against the center divot of his chest. "Well, if anyone can right the estate, it is you, Dom. You've been holding Vinehill together for ages— doing the hard work of running an estate like that—so taking over Kirkmere Abbey should be an easy task for you." Her words slowed, thick, and she nuzzled her head along his shoulder, finding just the right spot to settle it.

"Your confidence in me is odd."

"Why?" The sleepy word was whispered with a deep breath.

"That you still have it in me. Even after I failed you."

Silence.

He waited, his breath held for seconds that dragged on far too long before he realized she'd fallen asleep. Too much brandy. Too much whisky. Her fingers had gone limp on her glass, and he tugged the tumbler from her grasp. He set it on the side table to his right, clinking it next to his own glass.

This he would also take. A thousand times over.

Karta sleeping on him, the shivers that had held onto her body long since dissipated. Karta peaceful, not teetering on that constant nervous edge she'd balanced along ever since she had woken in the abbey to see him. Karta without harsh words of his devastating betrayal on her lips.

This he would take.

It wasn't all of her. But he had time for that now.

As much time as she needed.

{ CHAPTER 9 }

She was slow to wake. Not like she usually did, with her eyes popping open, alert, the moment the slightest semblance of lucidness hit her.

No, she stayed in the state between sleep and awake, reveling in the warm comfort she was encased in.

Warm, safe comfort. Where she was always meant to be. Home. Home in a cocoon of strength.

Strength.

Damn.

Domnall. Domnall's arms were about her. His cocoon. His strength.

And yet still, she fought opening her eyes. She wanted this as long as possible, selfish though it may be. For once he found out the truth of her, she'd never have a moment like this again.

He moved beneath her and she realized how fully she was on top of him. Somewhere during the night he'd shifted them, leaning back in the corner of the settee for support with a leg long on the cushion. She'd draped herself fully along his body.

So fully she could feel a rather large, rather stiff reminder jutting into her abdomen of how intimately their bodies were entwined.

Yet still, she couldn't let go of the moment. Of the warmth.

Domnall cleared his throat, his hand moving along her back.

Karta refused to look up at him, keeping her face buried in his lawn shirt just above the cut of his waistcoat, her voice a whisper just in case he was still asleep. "Dom?"

"Yes?"

"I lied."

"About what?"

"I did think of you."

He didn't answer for a torturous moment. Maybe he was talking in his sleep.

Then his chest lifted in a heavy breath.

"When?"

"All the time." She braved the tilt of her chin, her eyes upward to see his face. "Every day. In moments of happiness. In moments of sadness. In moments of nothingness. All the time. I wished you were by my side all the time."

Without a word, he dragged her body upward, his lips meeting hers in a brutal, searing kiss. A kiss that she'd imagined thousands of times over.

A kiss that would break her.

Destroy everything between them.

She jerked away from him, her palms flat on his chest as she pushed herself upward.

His hands were quick to her upper arms, stopping her motion. "Why do you flinch?"

"I—I don't flinch."

"You flinch when we are close. You want me—then you push away."

She stared down at him, at the confusion in his dark blue eyes.

Confusion she couldn't abate. She didn't dare tell him that she pushed away because of what she'd become. That whatever they started would never be finished once he knew the truth.

"I don't pu—"

A sharp knock on the door interrupted her words. A knock she was ridiculously grateful for.

She scrambled upright as he released her arms, untangling her legs from his. Gaining her feet, she smoothed down the front of her rumpled dress as she left the drawing room to answer the door. Theodora jumped up from her spot by the fireplace and was at her bare heels.

She took a breath to steady herself as she reached for the door. With any luck, it was one of Domnall's men at the door and she could avoid conversation with Domnall for the rest of the morning. The entire day if she was even luckier. Maybe he was needed back at the abbey and she would be granted a reprieve.

She opened the door with far too much haste, not even bothering to glance out the side windows that flanked the door.

No—no, no, no.

Her feet shuffled involuntarily backward, her grip on the door handle the only thing stopping her from backing far across the foyer.

"Karta, what are you doing answering the door? Why is no one tending the stables?" Her eldest stepson, now the current Viscount Leviton, stepped past her, stomping the

snow off his boots. Freezing wet droplets landed on her bare toes.

She peeked past her stepson. There wasn't another soul. He'd travelled here alone?

Karta closed the door and spun back to him, her look shifting between the drawing room entryway and her stepson removing his great coat and shaking it. More frozen droplets on her toes. "George, what are you doing here? And alone?"

"That is the lackluster greeting I get?"

Domnall picked that moment to appear in the doorway of the drawing room.

Panic spiked deep in her gut and her toes curled into the floor in a weak attempt to not leap in front of Domnall and push him back into the drawing room to hide him away from her stepson.

George's eyes glanced to Domnall, dismissing him before he even saw him. But then his hands on his great coat froze and his look jerked back to Domnall, taking in his size. "Who is this?"

Karta stepped between the two men and Theodora flanked Domnall, her wary big eyes not leaving George. "George, this is Lord Kirkmere of Kirkmere Abbey across the glen. Domnall, this is Lord Leviton, my stepson."

George's eyes squinted at Domnall. "And just what, exactly, is Lord Kirkmere doing in my home?"

His home?

Karta bit her tongue. Of course the fop would consider this his house. He considered everything his. He had since the day she'd met him.

A frown captured her face. "Maggie—my maid, do you remember her? She is deathly sick and I went to Lord Kirkmere for assistance two nights past. He had a doctor and Maggie brought to the abbey where she could be taken care of properly."

George looked around. "Properly? Where is the staff I pay for?"

She bit her tongue harder, nearly drawing blood. It was her thirds that paid for the staff. George had made sure of that fact when he'd kicked her out of the Leviton family home.

She clasped her hands in front of her. "They are with their families for Christmastide. It's why I had to fetch help. I couldn't get the stable doors open to get one of the mares out to reach the doctor on my own."

"You gave the staff Christmastide off while Maggie was sick?"

"She wasn't sick days ago when they left. I presumed we would be fine, and then the storm hit and trapped us here. I am quite certain Maggie would have died had Lord Kirkmere and his men not helped us."

The thin set of George's mouth went tight and he looked past her at Domnall. "So why are you two not at the abbey?"

Karta flipped her hand up into the air between them. "We came back here to fetch some of my and Maggie's items, as it seems her recovery will take several days." She spun around to Domnall, the desperate look on her face begging him not to say a word. "Would you please be so kind as to fetch the bag I packed in my room above—the

third door on the left—while I gather the rest of Maggie's items?"

"Of course." Domnall inclined his head to George then looked to his deerhound. "Stay." He moved to the staircase, disappearing into the corridor above.

Karta waited until she heard the door of her room creak open and she turned back to George. "What are you doing here, George?"

He'd removed his gloves and hat, and his bare fingers ran across the thick pomade slicking his blond curly hair tight to his scalp. "I'm here for you, Karta."

Her eyebrows drew together. "What? Here for me?"

"Exactly, here for you. Enough time has passed since father died. Don't tell me you weren't expecting a visit from me."

"A visit…" Her words trailed off, her tongue at a loss for words as her stomach started to churn in earnest. "It's Christmastide, George. Shouldn't you be with your family? Your brothers. Your *wife*? Your *children*?"

He waved his hand in the air. "The bat doesn't care naught where I am, Christmastide or not. And it is time I took a present for myself."

Her head shook slowly, understanding every word he said yet still trying to fight the many grotesque layers of insinuations in his words. "A present—"

Domnall's heavy footsteps on the staircase cut her words.

She looked up to him and he held a plump valise up. Where he had found it or what he had put in it so quickly, she hadn't a clue, as she hadn't packed a single thing.

"Your bag, Karta." Domnall stepped down the last few stairs and set it next to the door.

George moved to stand in front of Domnall. "On further reflection, I was remiss in not thanking you for the assistance with what should have been my responsibility, Lord Kirkmere. And now that I have arrived, it only makes sense for Karta to stay here with me at the dower house, so her bag will not be necessary."

Domnall stood straight, his words slow as his head tilted to the side. "But you have no staff."

"I will recall them."

"That will take days for how they are scattered throughout the countryside." Domnall looked over his shoulder through the left side window by the door and poked his thumb in the air. "Your cook, alone, is a three days carriage ride from here."

"You seem to know much of the workings of my dower house," George said.

"I know the area." Domnall shrugged. "I must insist that you join us at Kirkmere Abbey."

"I'm sure Karta can make a meal or two if necessary."

Domnall stepped around George and aligned himself next to Karta. "I'm also sure that Karta would want to be at Maggie's bedside as she recovers. She has been nowhere but there these last days."

The left side of George's mouth pulled back into a sneer. "A loyal employer."

"The most." Domnall nodded. "I am sure you agree that the Maggie's health is paramount and Karta needs to be at her side. So I insist. You will come to Kirkmere, at

least until the staff arrives back here from their celebrations and will be able to attend to you. Unless you can handle the house and meals on your own."

Karta stifled a guffaw—George handling anything with his own two hands was preposterous. Once the laugh was swallowed back, she glanced at George, a strained smile on her face.

Her stepson's mouth twisted in a grumble as he glared at Domnall, but then he nodded.

Thank the heavens.

Now she just had to make sure George was never in a room alone with Domnall. For if he was—if the two spoke—it was all over for her.

Domnall would never look at her the same again.

{ CHAPTER 10 }

Karta stared at Theodora's tail swinging back and forth, brushing the drifts of snow on either side of the skinny path that had been worn from the stables to the abbey.

They walked single file, Theodora leading the way, Domnall directly behind her after he slid in front of George at the last second before the trail through the snow slipped down to shoulder's width. George had been forced to the rear.

Much to her pleasure, though she didn't imagine it was sitting well with George. She hadn't bothered to look back to see his indignation, not that she could see him past the wall of Domnall—George was half his width, scrawny, even, in comparison. She truly had been surrounded by fragile men these past years and she hadn't even realized it.

"But before inheriting the title, I was the steward at Vinehill Castle in Stirlingshire," Domnall said, his footsteps heavy behind her.

He'd kept up strained, polite conversation with George the entire way back to Kirkmere Abbey and for how silent Domnall usually was, she knew he did it for her. To take the awkwardness of George's sudden appearance off her shoulders—when what he really wanted to do was capture her alone and ask her why in the hell her stepson would show up at her door on Christmas eve day. She could feel that question burning in Domnall with every stiff motion he made near her, with every singeing glare he gave her.

"Vinehill castle?" George asked. His voice went louder to reach past Domnall to her. "The Vinehill men—those were your failed engagements, Karta, weren't they?"

She stepped into the clearing of snow around the rear door of the abbey and nodded as Domnall stepped past her to open the door. "They were."

George's smarmy look locked onto her, his smile curling the edges of his thin lips. "One betrothed dead and one betrothal broken, if I remember correctly? You were lucky my father took you after all the scandal of both of those."

Domnall jerked the door open and George stepped in front of Karta, cutting her off and stepping into the abbey first.

George looked to Domnall as he passed him. "So you were part of that merry band of Vinehill men who wreaked terror on the innocent maids in the land?"

His jaw flexing, Domnall ushered her into the abbey and the slightest squint came to his eyes as he looked at George. "Not exactly." He closed the door behind him with admirable control. "I am lucky to have worked for the Marquess of Vinehill. I was an orphan and he took me in, raised me. Gave me every opportunity to become more than my circumstances allowed. I am fortunate in all that I was taught, as I am well-versed in running an estate thanks to him. That knowledge will be a tremendous help here, as Kirkmere Abbey has much to be righted."

"What a charming story." Sarcasm thick in his high-pitched voice, George removed his coat and dropped it and his gloves in a heap on the floor as he looked around the small vestibule in the rear of the abbey.

Domnall stepped in front of him, pointing down to George's outerwear on the floor. "What are you doing?"

George looked around, his eyebrows arched in disbelief. "You don't have someone to collect our gear?"

"Whether I have someone or not isn't the point. Don't disrespect my home by dumping your sopping coat onto my floor. Pick up the jacket, Lord Leviton."

For long, agonizing seconds both of the men glared at each other, neither moving a muscle. George bolstered by an inherited sense of pomp and privilege. Domnall not needing to be bolstered by anything—he already was the better man in every which way that mattered.

Her breath held, Karta was just about to pick up George's coat so the situation wouldn't come to blows when George coughed and looked away.

Grumbling under his breath, George turned around to pick up his overcoat and gloves. "I have a mind to tell you exactly—"

Karta jumped between them, her voice loud and drowning out George's words. "Dom, it looks like Theodora is famished, but she isn't about to go anywhere without you."

He looked down at his deerhound, his lips pursing. "She hasn't eaten since yesterday."

"And it was a long trek for her back and forth from the dower house."

"Wait." George jerked upright with his coat in his hands. "You two spent the night together at the dower house?"

A high-pitched laugh burst out of her mouth. "Don't be silly, George. Theodora accompanied me to the dower house last evening."

"So you spent the night there but he did not?" George's finger flung out at Domnall.

She nodded, her eyebrows lifting in her best attempt to look at him like he was mad as the lie slid easily off her tongue. "Of course."

"But you have been nowhere but at your maid's side, I thought," George said.

"Except for last night—the dark closed in so quickly on me that I didn't dare set back to Kirkmere in the ink of the night. Domnall came to make certain I was well and collect me this morning."

Domnall cleared his throat, his mouth pulling to the side. "Please excuse me, then. The hound is hungry." His look rested on her for a long moment. He knew exactly what she was doing and he didn't approve.

Without the slightest glance at George, he reached down and scratched Theodora's ears. With a long look back to Karta, the hound followed Domnall down the center hallway for a few steps and then they turned to the left, disappearing down the stairwell to the kitchens.

She waited until the echo of Domnall's steps was swallowed by the ancient stones and then she whipped around to George. "What do you think you're doing, George? This is Domnall's home and you come in and manifest this rudeness?" Her hand motioned to his coat draped over his left arm. "He has a good mind to kick you out into the snow and then where will you be?"

A sneer lifted the right side of his mouth. "I'll be back at the dower house with you."

Her arms clasped across her chest. "It's not going to happen, George."

"Maybe not today, but you did say your maid was on the mend." His head tilted to the side. "She should be ready to come to the dower house and tend to us in a day or two."

"She almost just died, George. She is not going to be up to waiting on you hand and foot for quite some time."

"Then you will just have to do my bidding for her." He stepped toward her—too close. "You must know that I've thought of little else since the last time I saw you—the situation we found you in." A snake smile curled his lips. "Truly, how could I not obsess?"

Her gut tightened into a tiny, hard ball. "How could you not obsess?" She leaned toward him, her eyes level with his. "You're a grown man, George. You have a wife and children. Too many mistresses to count. That is how you don't obsess."

She reached out and plucked his coat and gloves from him. "Your coat and gloves will be in the front hall. I'll find Domnall's butler and he can show you to an appropriate room."

"Ordering about his butler? You've made yourself at home here."

Karta turned away, moving toward the hallway.

"You're here for him, aren't you?" His words came out in a hiss.

She stopped, looking over her shoulder at him. "I don't know what you're talking about."

"I couldn't even fathom it when I first saw him—he's so…" His gave an exaggerated shudder. "So large. So uncouth."

"Whatever you're thinking, George, you're wrong."

George shook his head to himself, his tiny eyes going to pinpricks as he stared at her. "He doesn't know." A revelation, he said the words in a whisper.

She pretended not to have heard him. "If you'll excuse me, I do need to go and tend to Maggie." She started to stalk away from him.

He grabbed her wrist, stopping her escape. "He doesn't know, does he? Doesn't know about you."

"George—

Abrupt laughter barked from his mouth, cutting her off. "Play the innocent all you want Karta—I know what you are."

She couldn't look at him for the bile that chased up her throat. "George, I must tend to Maggie, excuse me."

She shoved off of him and turned, her steps quick down the hall as she ignored his snicker trailing in the air behind her.

She needed George out of Kirkmere Abbey.

The sooner the better.

{ CHAPTER 11 }

The rest of Christmas Eve day had passed and she'd managed to avoid both Domnall, and more importantly, George, by stashing herself away in Maggie's room.

Karta stood from her seat by her maid's bedside and stretched her arms high above her head, looking out the window into the darkness of the evening. The moon still big and bright and reflecting off the snow made it look like twilight, even though it'd been dark for hours. Her spine cracked in three places with the stretch, indicative of the many hours she'd sat in there today.

Maggie had been in and out of fever the entire day. The stretches of lucid moments stretched longer and longer, though the doctor said she could slip back into full fever at any moment. Karta had tended Maggie's head with cool wet cloths and set spoonful after spoonful of broth to her lips. There were moments were Maggie had managed to slurp the broth into her mouth, and that had buoyed Karta's spirits more than anything. At least she wouldn't lose her only friend. Fate couldn't be that cruel, could it?

Her gaze remained on the long expanse of snow rolling along the sheep field as she twisted her torso, loosening the muscles along her sides. She needed bed and she needed to eat before she fell into exhaustion herself.

If she could just make it down to the kitchens without encountering anyone, she would count the day a success.

What her stepson hoped to accomplish here in Badenoch—if she'd taken his insinuation this morning exactly as she was sure he intended—was beyond the pale.

Just because George knew her secret didn't give him carte blanche to her body—something he'd clearly decided in the last six months he had every right to. He'd always made it known that he was entitled to anything and everything—from every scrub brush of the estate to the smallest crumb in the kitchens—and apparently, he had deemed himself entitled to her. Even though he had a wife and several mistresses, now he thought to own her as well.

Her tongue curled at the thought. Of his boney fingers reaching for her. Touching her. His always sour breath in her face.

She shuddered, her look going to the glowing embers in the fireplace.

Thank goodness Domnall had the good sense to extract her from the situation at the dower house. He always had been adept at stepping in at the right moment. Now she just had to figure out how to extract herself even further from George's slimy clutches.

She could find a cottage on the far coast of the Isle of Skye—too far of a journey for even George. But she would need her thirds to afford that, and by using it, George would be able to follow her if he became determined. Plus, she couldn't disappear until Maggie was well enough to travel with her.

She could travel back to her father's home, but George was such a frequent guest there that she would be serving herself up on a fine silver platter to him.

Or she could stay at the dower house and attempt to shut down his advances from there. It would be much easier if the full staff were present.

She wasn't sure how far George would dare press her—but what she did know was that he'd never heard the word no in his life.

That made him dangerous.

So for now, her best—only—course was to stay at the abbey.

She moved away from Maggie's bed, stopping at the closed door and listening. Not a sound in the hallway. Hopefully it was late enough that everyone had retired.

Slipping into the corridor, she pulled Maggie's door closed and passed into the shadow of the sconce at the end of the hall toward the stairs. She made it down the steps and past the drawing room, library, study, dining hall and moved down the rear staircase to the kitchens. The door to the study had been ajar, a fire lit inside, but she didn't stop to see who was in there. She most certainly didn't want to encounter George, and she wasn't yet ready to tackle Domnall.

Not yet.

He'd been a gracious enough host to George, but in every interaction she'd witnessed between the two men, she could see under Domnall's strained smile that he wanted to crush George's skull.

Domnall had restraint like no one she'd ever known.

Stepping into the kitchen, she moved to stand next to the large worn center table and reached for a chunk of bread. Tearing off a piece, she popped it into her mouth.

Still warm. Cook must have just taken it from the oven before retiring.

Karta turned, leaning against the table as she tore chunks and popped them into her mouth. Chewing silently, she stared at the glowing coals on the hearth.

"I thought I heard a little mouse scurrying about."

Karta jumped, spinning around.

George advanced directly at her, stepping in front of her and blocking her path to the doorway. He wore only a night robe on his thin frame, the skin of his chest peeking above the top fold of cloth and his feet were bare on the stone floor of the kitchen.

"G—" She choked on the piece of bread stuck in her throat, coughing, slapping her chest until it wedged free and she managed to swallow it. "George. I thought the household was asleep."

"It would bode well for us."

"For us?" Her eyebrow cocked at him. "What do you mean, us?"

"Us. Don't try to deny it, Karta. I knew it from the moment father brought you into Leviton Hall. You want me. You've always wanted me. I saw it in how you looked at me. How you would watch me. I am so much younger, so much more vital than father. There's no shame in admitting it." He took another step closer, closing the distance between them. "And now that he's dead, you can have me."

He moved in so swiftly, so aggressively, that she didn't have time to react. His lips on her mouth, crushing hers. The sour of his tongue mixing with the stench of cognac about him, invading her nostrils. His hand griped her right wrist, twisting it behind her until the bread fell from her hand.

He pulled his mouth slightly back, inhaling, his nostril flaring. "And I know how you like it. I know exactly what to—"

She wedged her left hand up, slapping him. Hard. The force of it tearing his face away from hers.

He sucked in a wicked breath, releasing her hand as he took a step backward.

"You're delusional, George. I don't want you. I never wanted you. I never once looked at you like that."

"Not want me?" His hand went to his cheek, rubbing as his mouth twisted in fury. "You've always wanted me, so why not now?"

Karta edged along the table, her fingertips moving across the edge of the roughhewn wood, trying to gain a clear angle to the doorway. Run, scream, whatever it took to get away from her stepson's madness.

George's look went down to her fingers moving along the table and his eyes went wide, rage flashing in his green irises with his lips snarling. "So, it is that brute, isn't it? Just like I thought."

She froze in place. As much as she wanted to escape George's clutches, she wasn't about to let him disparage Domnall. Not in his home. Not ever.

A growl like she'd never heard from her own lips set thunder into her words. "He's not a brute."

"He's a giant oaf."

Both of her arms swung out, her palms smacking him hard in the chest. He faltered two steps backward. "He's

gentle and respects me and he's a thousand times the man you are."

George's hands whipped up and he snatched her wrists in the air, going to his toes to lean over her, snarling. "Then I'll tell him—I'll tell him what you are. Hide it all you want. But he doesn't know, for if he did he wouldn't give you the slightest glance."

She bit her lip. "You cannot."

"You think I'm not respectful? I think I am." He threw her wrists down. "To prove it, I'll give you one day. Think over what you truly want in life. What is actually attainable for you now in your situation. Give me what is mine and I keep my mouth shut. Or don't, and I tell him the truth and ruin you in his eyes. It's your choice." He took another step backward, his head nodding. "But I do imagine, either way, you'll end up in my bed at the dower house, Karta."

"You don't have a bed at the dower house, George."

A smirk snaked onto his lips. "I do now. One way or another."

He left the room, the sickening stench of his pomade wafting out in the air behind him.

{ CHAPTER 12 }

Foregoing knocking, Domnall opened the door of the Leviton dower house and peeked his head inside.

Silence.

For the quiet stillness, he wouldn't have believed Karta had come back here again if not for one of his horses from Kirkmere resting in the stable. She had left the saddle on her mare, which told him she didn't plan to stay at the dower house for an extended period of time.

Or so he hoped.

He liked her under his roof. Safe. In a place where the leering looks of that idiot stepson of hers would be stomped into oblivion before they became action.

Domnall stepped into the foyer from the quiet air of the morning and quickly walked down the center hall of the house. All the rooms were empty. A floorboard creaked above him and he reversed course and went up the stairs.

He pushed the door to Karta's room wide open, only to find the top of her body buried deep in the wardrobe in the far corner of the room.

She'd already changed into a delightful plum concoction that draped over her curves far too enticingly. Leaning against the doorframe, he watched her backside shift about for a long moment. Selfish ogling, but he wasn't about to apologize for it. "It's Christmas day. What are ye doing here, Karta?"

She jumped with a squeak and spun to him, her hand flat on her chest. "Dom. Blast your damn stealth." The words came with a screech.

"Apologies." He couldn't hide the smile on his face. "What are ye doing here, Karta?"

She pointed over her shoulder. "I actually did need some clothing to change into, since my valise that you brought back with us only contained a pillow."

He shrugged with a grin. "It was the closest thing to snatch when I was up here. It took me too long to find the bag, so I grabbed the first thing I could find to plump it up. I wasn't about to leave ye alone with Lord Leviton for a moment longer than necessary."

A grin lifted her cheeks. "I presumed as much."

"Ye scared me when I couldn't find you in the abbey, what with Leviton lurking about. Ye could have sent me for your items—or Rory could have come."

She shrugged. "There wasn't a need. I saw Colin take George out for hunting and I thought it was a good time to escape."

"Escape from me or escape from him?"

"Him." A crooked smile crossed her lips and her look shifted to the side wall. "And maybe you."

He straightened, his fingers curling into fists. "That bastard wants exactly what I think he wants from you, doesn't he?"

She inhaled, her chest lifting high as her eyes met his. She nodded. "Yes."

He turned and his fist smashed into the frame of the door. Instant and ferocious. His arm flying before the slightest consideration of control could spark in his brain.

Pain shocked up his arm.

Worth it.

Worth every sharp twinge quaking along his bones.

"Dom." Her breathless word floated through the air thick with rage surrounding him.

The fear in the word—fear for him, not for herself—filtered in through the red that had just flooded his mind and he shook his head. Shook sanity back into his brain.

He didn't lose control. Not like this. Not over anything.

Anything, except Karta.

With her, his control was always on the edge, always a thin glass pane, splintering and cracking bit by bit, waiting to break at the slightest vibration.

He seethed in a breath and then turned to her, shaking the shock from his arm.

"Why do ye not just send the cad out on his arse?"

"It's not that easy."

"No? You owe him something?"

Her head shook, her mouth clamping shut.

Dammit.

He'd had enough.

Whatever the reason that caused her to push him away, to run from him again and again, he needed to know. Now. Before her need to remove herself from him set her into a situation with George that would irrevocably hurt her.

He attempted to set the tone of his voice even with only marginal success. "And why did ye need to escape from me?"

Her eyes went wide. "I don't really want to escape from you, Dom. Don't think that."

"Yet you did. Why?"

Her lips pursed. "It is more that I didn't want to face you, not today. Not alone."

"Why not?"

Her head went down, her fingers twisting together in front of her belly. "I've been avoiding it since you brought me into the abbey and I was hoping for just another day— one more day, especially because it's Christmas. I was going to grab a new dress and be bright and cheery and take everything I could from this day with you. I just needed this one day."

"A day for what?"

Her head lifted and her golden brown eyes pinned him. "A day before I told you the truth."

{ CHAPTER 13 }

He reeled slightly backward. Not enough to force a step. But he reeled.

Almost unperceivable. But she saw it. She saw everything about him. She always had.

And Domnall didn't reel. He didn't sway. He was a block of granite that time and rain and ice could not touch.

Exactly why she didn't want to have to do this. Tell him.

He didn't take a moment to clear his throat, just barreled forward, his blue eyes piercing her. "Whatever it is, whatever truth you've been keeping from me, Karta, ye need to tell me. Now."

Her eyes closed, her breath shaking into her chest as she tried to manifest strength she didn't think she had.

Her eyelids cracked, her look steady on him. "When I told you I was different now, Dom, it is about who—about what I've become. About the things that happened with my husband."

"Ye told me he didn't hurt you, Karta." His feet stopped, rage quaking deep in his words.

Her hand flew up between them. "No. He didn't. Not intentionally."

He took another step toward her, moving within arm's length. "Then why do I see shame in your eyes? You're fighting something. Hiding something."

"He died upon me, Dom." The words flew out of her mouth, bitter spikes she shot into the air. "He died on me. In bed."

Domnall froze, his eyes squinting at her. "He died with you in bed?" The words were slow, agonized.

Three quick breaths that made her head light and words blurted from her in a rush. A rush to get this over and done with. A rush to the pain that would cut across her chest when the disgust would appear in his eyes.

Yet there wasn't anything she could do now except tell Domnall before George did. "Yes. On me. In the act. He was on top of me and then he just stopped. Collapsed onto me. And I started screaming. Screaming and screaming. And his sons ran into the room."

"Bloody hell, Karta."

"There's more." Her eyes closed, her face tortured. "You have to understand, my husband rarely came to my bed—only when he was between mistresses. He didn't want more children. His line of heirs was well established." She stopped, taking a deep breath that shook her body. "He had tied my wrists and ankles to the bedposts. Wide. He'd always told me that was how he enjoyed it the most. With me lashed in place, captive under him." Her closed eyes scrunched tight as heat spread across her neck, her face. "And there was a riding crop curled tight in his hand. But he never hurt me with any of it—not truly—so I accommodated his wishes."

Silence.

So much so she had to crack her eyes open to make sure he hadn't quietly backed out of the room.

He hadn't gone anywhere. Hadn't moved a muscle. His stare still slicing her in two.

Then recognition flickered in his blue eyes. "Dammit—his sons walked in on that?" His hand ran across his face and he shook his head. "That bastard—George—walked in on that?"

She nodded, her eyes fully opening, though she couldn't look directly at him any longer. Couldn't witness the revulsion in his eyes. She stared at her delicately lined secretary in the corner of the room. A desk that haunted her every day, for she had no one to write to.

For how much she wanted to crumple in that moment, turn into a puddle and slip under the floorboards to hide from Domnall, she knew he had to know everything—*everything*—of that scene. She had to tell him before George did.

She swallowed hard. "They had to peel him off of me. All three of his sons were in the room." The burn of the humiliation had fully flooded the back of her neck, spreading into her scalp and making her hair stand on end. "He was naked. I was naked except for my stockings. The riding crop was still…in me…he liked that. I was tied down and couldn't move…couldn't hide…" She exhaled, the moment in time washing over her again in brutal mortification. "They saw everything. Everything of their father. Everything of me. And the damnation was swift and complete."

"Karta—"

"It's the real reason I was banished to Badenoch. You can imagine what happened after they found me like that.

They blamed me for his death and then told people what had happened." She inhaled deeply, attempting to solidify her spine against the repulsion she would find in him when she looked up.

A beaten smile pulled her cheeks back. "No one will touch me. Not a friend. Not a relative. Not another suitor. I'm a killer and a sordid whore, and his sons made sure every contact they had knew that fact—and then the gossipmongers took over from there."

"So you ran? You didn't fight it?"

Her look whipped up to him. "There's no fighting it, Dom. It happened. There's nothing to deny."

"Let me get this correct." His jaw flexed. "A man—far too old and in no condition for taking his young wife to bed—ties her up, enjoys an accoutrement with her, then dies on top of her, and she's the villain?"

Her chest tightened.

She told him. Now she needed him to walk away. To not stretch the pain of this into minutes, into hours.

Her fingers lifted, swiping at a tear that had escaped her lower lashes. "I'm a wretched whore. A killer. A pariah in society. It is how the world works."

"Not my world." His voice was a low rumble, raw. "Not when you are the one destroyed by it."

Another tear slipped to her cheek. "Dom, no."

"Don't tell me you believe them." He took one step toward her, collapsing the space between them to nothing. "Tell me you don't believe those bastard Leviton boys. For that's what they are. Sniveling, weak little boys."

Her throat closed, unable to let air or words through.

His hand lifted, his thumb caressing her cheek, wiping away the wetness before his fingers curled around her neck. "I am with you, Karta. No matter what ye believe. No matter what the world thinks. I am with you. It's always been so. It will always be so."

Air broke through her lungs that she expelled in a gasp. A gasp that was swallowed by his mouth on hers. His body pressing into hers.

It took her a full minute to realize he hadn't walked away. Hadn't looked at her with disgust. With scorn.

He'd only looked at her with rage at the injustice of what she'd suffered.

With love.

It didn't matter to him. It didn't matter what happened. What she did. What the world thought she was.

It didn't matter.

He was with her.

And he wasn't going anywhere.

His arms clamped around her body, swallowing her into the mass of him and her arms snaked up, tentative, almost as though if she touched him he would jump away. Disappear.

Her fingers wrapped around his neck, the cords of muscles under his skin twitching under her touch. He didn't step back, didn't push her away. If anything, the kiss deepened, his tongue exploring her, tasting her, drinking in the essence of her.

He pulled up slightly, his hand cupping the side of her face. "I let this happen. I should have been there at the ball.

I never should have let ye fall onto this path that has taken such joy from your eyes."

She stared up at him. At the regret palpitating in his dark blue eyes.

His other hand lifted and he set her face between his hands. "It's Christmas and I need a gift from you."

"A gift?"

"Yes." His eyes closed for a long second before his lashes opened, his gaze intent on her. "Give me you. Give me forgiveness for not acting sooner. Give me a chance to love ye like you were meant to be loved. Like I have always loved you."

His words shook her to her soul, sending every nerve in her body to fire. A smile lifted her mouth as she tightened her hold on his neck. "And what will you give me?"

"Everything. Everything I am and will ever be."

Her breath stopped in her chest. "I don't think I can accept that."

His eyebrows cocked.

"Unless you accept the very same thing from me."

She pulled herself up to his mouth, kissing him with the very depths of her soul.

He yanked her body hard into his and his hand rolled down her spine, rounding her backside. It sent tangs of desire deep into her gut, craving all his body could do to hers.

Her heels flicked up and she took a step backward, dragging him with her. One step. Two. Her calves touched the side of her bed.

Domnall yanked his head away. "No. We stop this now."

"What?" The word came breathless from her throat.

He shook his head. "I can't."

"Yes, you can." She went higher on her toes, her fingers digging into the back of his neck. "I'm not the innocent virgin I once was. I—"

"No. I will have no problem taking ye, Karta." A slow smile spread across his face. "I'm stopping because I'm taking you back to the abbey."

"Why?"

"One, ye don't cook and I'm starving. Two, I'm not going to let you out of my sight until springtime. Every time you're alone in this snow ye manage to get tangled into some mishap."

She couldn't argue that.

"Three, and most important—there's no one here to marry us."

Her head snapped back. "Marry us?"

"Yes. I want ye, Karta. All of you, always." His blue eyes pierced her, the love he'd always had for her resonating deep in his look. "I can choose what—where—my life is now. And it's you—you are my life, if you'll have me."

The thudding in her chest beat so hard, so loud in her head, she could barely form the words to her tongue.

She nodded. "I will have you, Dom. Always."

{ Chapter 14 }

He stood next to her in front of the doctor with Rory and Bailey in the drawing room as witnesses. Thank the heavens they were in Scotland. The doctor was willing. Karta was willing. So he would make her his wife in this very moment.

It had been torture, the ride back to the abbey. Watching the sway of her body on the horse. His heart quickening every time she'd looked over her shoulder at him, a smile—hesitant and genuine and hopeful—on her lips. The very smile he remembered from years ago before they were parted. The smile that held the world, the future, in its depths.

But for this—Karta properly in his bed—or not so properly—he could clamp down on his straining cock.

This was more important than anything—joining them for the rest of times.

He grabbed her left hand, clasping her delicate fingers into his palm. Her skin was still cold from the ride. Something he would rectify just as soon as this doctor managed to get his cravat straightened and marry them.

One last blasted smoothing of his cravat and the doctor cleared his throat. "I've not done this before, so you will have to forgive me."

Domnall's head tilted to the doctor, keeping his voice in check. "Just the few words is all we need, good sir."

"Right." The doctor nodded. "Well then, face each other, I suppose."

Domnall turned to Karta and grabbed her right hand as well.

The doctor inclined his head. "Domnall Greyford do you take Karta Williamson to be your wife?"

"I will." So easy, the words from his mouth. Such a quick and simple trade for the only thing he'd ever wanted in his life.

The doctor turned to Karta. "Karta Williamson do you take Domnall Greyford to be your husband?"

She looked up at him, the golden flecks of honey in her brown eyes glowing, shining with love. "I will."

A crooked smile appeared on the doctor's face. "Well then, I suppose that is the whole of it? It seems as though there should be more—something akin to love, honor and obey, perhaps?"

"That will do." Domnall nodded to him. He'd witnessed enough quick Scottish weddings to know they'd done the most important part.

The doctor shook his head a bit, wanting to say more, but then he shrugged his shoulders. "I guess I then pronounce you man and wife."

Domnall's lips were on Karta's before the doctor finished his words.

"What the hell is going on here?" George's nasally voice filled the drawing room.

Domnall froze in place, his lips on Karta's as he inhaled a deep breath. If he didn't calm in that instant, he was going to injure Lord Leviton so grievously the man would be in an asylum the rest of his days.

Control intact, Domnall lifted his head from Karta, noting her wide eyes before looking to George. "It is none of your concern, Lord Leviton."

George dumped the two pheasants he had strung over his shoulder onto the floor of the drawing room, their carcasses thudding onto the floorboards. "Don't tell me I have no concern, you blasted oaf. You're manhandling my property."

Domnall exploded. "Property—"

"My lord—" With his hands high, the doctor tried to intervene, stepping toward George.

"You don't know what she is." A sneer pulled George's face tight as he pushed the doctor aside and advanced at Domnall. "You've let this murderous whore into your home and I have every right to her and whatever she thinks she's doing here." As quick as a snake he snatched Karta's arm, yanking her away from Domnall.

Her fingers jerked out of Domnall's grasp.

Too far.

Before she lost another step toward George, Domnall stepped in front of Karta and slammed his fist into George's face.

Brutal, savage. A punch so vicious it cracked bones and sliced skin.

Crushing the man—he didn't care. The bastard had dared to touch his wife.

George flew backward with a squeal, his shoulder hitting the doorframe and sending him flailing. He landed

on the dead birds, blood from his nose splattering across the wall, the floor.

Domnall followed him, ready to finish the ass, when Karta's hand clamped onto his upper arm.

"Dom. No. Just let him go. He's not worth it." Her whisper, soft and pleading, broke through the fiery rage filling his veins.

It wasn't enough.

With a high swing, he brought his fist down.

He stopped it.

An inch from the sniveling bastard's head. He stopped.

She was right. George wasn't worth it. And Karta was worth stopping for.

His fist opened and he grabbed the fold of George's collar. Stepping over him, he dragged the man to the front foyer. He opened the door and picked George fully up, throwing him down the stone steps leading up to the abbey.

George tumbled, splaying into the bank of snow that lined the cleared pathway, his face straight into the cold ice of it.

"You're walking away because of my wife, Lord Leviton. She's the only reason you're alive, so you will give her the respect she is due." The words seethed though his clenched teeth. "If I hear of the slightest rumor that you or your brothers ever speak on her name again, I will come for you. If you ever set foot in these lands again, I will come for you."

Domnall moved out onto the top step, leaning out over Leviton, the wrath of a thousand demons raging in his words. "And when I come, I will have no control and Karta will not stop me. You only get one warning, you cowardly sorry dung of a man. You have one hour to vacate these lands."

Without a word, George scrambled to his feet, his arms punching through the collapsing snow again and again until he found enough ground to push up from. Onto his feet, he slipped on the icy bricks of the walkway, barely maintaining balance. His hands clasped against his bloody nose and he skidded his way through the snow toward the stables, blood droplets trailing in the white drifts behind him.

Watching the pathetic bastard retreat, Domnall felt the few strains of control he'd managed starting to snap.

The man touched Karta. Touched his *wife*.

His fingers itched against his palm. Hell, he was going to follow the ass and finish him.

A hand, still cool, wrapped along the side of his neck from behind.

"Dom." Karta's voice was soft, cracking. "Step back. Close the door. Rory is already on his way out the side door to the stables. He'll see George gone."

Domnall couldn't move. Couldn't move until George disappeared around the corner of the abbey.

Her fingers curled along the bare skin of his neck. "Step back, Dom."

The fury still palpitating in his veins, he turned around to her, afraid of what he would find. Afraid she would now see him as the monster everyone always suspected him to be.

His look landed on her face, on her brown eyes.

Awe. Pride. Lust

All of it, entwined with love in her eyes.

She was home. Home with him.

All he ever wanted. And he wasn't about to leave her side for anything.

{ CHAPTER 15 }

He turned to her, this warrior of a man, framed by the front door and the landscape of cold white beyond. His muscles strained under his coat, his body shaking with rage. The hard cut of his jawline—solid, immovable, impenetrable stone.

Strength she'd never seen him allow unbridled.

Unbridled for her.

She wanted him like never before.

He hadn't turned for but a moment before she crashed into him, her lips finding his. Remnants of his raw anger sent him on the attack, bruising her lips, crushing her body to his.

She took it all, took everything he always was. Because now he was hers.

He lifted her up, walking—stalking up the stairs as his mouth stayed ravenous on hers and he moved straight to his room.

She realized the boorishness of it—leaving the doctor and Bailey standing with their gaping mouths in the foyer below—but she was no force against it.

This—her and Domnall together—had needed to happen for so long there was no more denying it, no more delaying it.

He crashed through the door to his chambers, slamming the door closed behind him.

The door bounced back open with the force, and he pulled his mouth away from her as he leaned against the door to close it. She reached past his shoulder to latch it.

"That took too bloody long," he exhaled in a long breath.

His hand shifted under her backside and she tightened her grip around his neck as she wedged her legs upward to wrap along his hip bones. "The wedding?"

"Yes—the wedding—smashing the entitlement off of George's face." The growl in his chest vibrated against her breasts. "The whole of it."

"Too long?" Her words came out breathless, her air mingling with his. "How is that possible? It was five minutes traded for a lifetime."

"Five minutes is too long when all I can think about is ripping the clothing off your body."

"You aren't about to woo me into bed?"

"We're not going to the bed. And you don't like to be wooed. You like my body hard against yours. You like action. You always have. And you'll like me turning us around and me taking you hard against the door."

A pang sparked in the depth of her, her core aching at his words, and a throaty laugh escaped from deep in her chest. "I think there's a reason I just married you."

"You love me?"

"Yes. But I love you because you're the only person in this world that has ever taken the time to know what I like. How I think. You have always seen me. Me beyond who my father is. Me beyond the pawn that I have been. To look past what others think of me." Her voice trailed off on her last words.

"No. I'll not have that, Karta." He walked over to the bed and plucked her body off his, then dropped her onto the side of the bed. He leaned over her, his voice a low roar. "I'll not have those words, that doubt from your lips ever again—do you understand?"

Without waiting for an answer, he turned from her, his fingers ripping through his cravat to loosen it and drag it free of his neck. Boots, coat, waistcoat, lawn shirt, trousers. He stripped down in front of her so quickly she didn't even have time to blink.

His bare backside to her, the glory of his skin, of his muscles taut, rippling along every hard curve of his body made her mouth water. Made her question how she was ever going to manage to please him for all his wonder.

Her hands went down to her boots and she tugged them off, then sat upright. She expelled a held breath. "I thought we weren't going to the bed."

He glanced over his shoulder at her. "I changed my mind."

Moving over to the tall dresser along the inner wall, he pulled free the top drawer. His fingers quick, he yanked out two long cravats of white cloth. "This should do." He walked over to the bed, stopping in front of her, his manhood large and engorged and directly at her eye level.

For all that her tongue was watering a moment ago, her mouth went dry, her core pounding with anticipation.

Her chin tilted up, her eyes wide. "Do for what?"

"Tying wrists to the bed."

Her head jerked back. "No, I—"

"Did you like it, Karta?" He leaned over her, his words low, dangerous. "Being tied up?"

"I don't—I don't know—"

"Did you like it?"

Her eyes closed for a long breath. "I…I didn't hate it."

"So I think you're going to like this." A smile, wanton, came to his face. "But I'm not tying you up. You're tying me."

"I—what?" Her eyes went wide.

"You're tying me up. Lashing me to the bed. You're going to be in complete control of me." He gave a slight shake of his head. "You were never meant to be tied down, Karta. You were always meant to be free. Your mind, your body, your soul."

"Dom, I don't know if I—"

"No—we're even in this—always. You've been tied to a bed. I want that same experience. I want you to do that to me. You are my match, my love, in every single way, and I don't want you to ever feel shame for what your life has brought you. So you do this and I can show you exactly how right this can be. How there is no shame in it."

He shoved one of the strips into her hand and he moved past her to lie back on the bed, setting his wrist next to the carved mahogany bedpost. His gaze landed on her, insistent as his voice went hard. "Now tie me up."

She stared at him for a long moment, unsure.

If she didn't trust him more than anything—trust him more than she trusted herself—she wouldn't have moved.

But she did.

Slowly, she crawled over his naked torso and weaved the cloth around the post, crossing his wrists several times and then back to the post. She tied a knot.

"It's tight."

She looked down at his face. "Too tight?"

His right cheek lifted with a wicked grin. "Perfectly tight."

The smallest smile came to her face and she moved over him to reach his left wrist. It only took her quick seconds to lash it to the other bedpost and her breath left her as she sat back on her heels on the bed.

Domnall spread out before her. Thick arms wide. His chest lifting in heavy breaths. The muscles along his abdomen twitching. The full length of his member, large and strong and straining upward against his belly. His dark blue eyes on fire, smoldering with wanting to attack her but not having the ability to.

Vulnerable.

He was absolutely under her control.

As much as she wanted to lift her skirts and slide down directly onto his engorged shaft, feel the length of him deep inside of her, she wasn't about to let this opportunity pass her. The odd sense of power. Of control.

She pushed herself to her toes and stood upright on the bed. The blue damask canopy of the tester bed still high above her, she stretched her arms up high in a long stretch, then shuffled to his legs. She slipped her toes between his legs, spreading his right leg wide, then his left.

Stepping between his legs, she lifted her skirts, reaching for the ribbon holding up the stocking on her right leg.

Tugging the ribbon loose, she slowly dragged the stocking downward, making sure to keep her skirts high, showing every speck of skin she revealed.

A groan rumbled in his chest. "Hell, Karta. You cannot do this to me."

"I can. And I am." She switched to her left leg, stripping down the other stocking even slower.

His legs curled around her ankles and she shook her head, a wicked smile on her lips as she kicked his calves wide again.

Her fingers went to the military row of brass buttons on her spencer and she flicked them free, pausing between each one. Watching his face. Watching the torture she was causing him. If he'd been free, he'd already be inside of her and riding her hard. And she would be loving it.

But this was much more fun.

She stripped back her jacket and loosened the white muslin shirt layered beneath it, pulling it up over her head. The air hit her arms and she dropped the shirt behind her with her spencer. Three buttons about her waist to loosen her heavy wool skirt and it dropped to the bed to puddle about his thighs.

Stepping backward out of the mess of cloth, she bent forward and stretched out to pick her skirt from his body, letting her knuckles graze his member as she lifted it from his body.

A gasp. A low and guttural gasp. He swallowed hard, his eyes closing for a long breath.

"Open your eyes, Dom."

His lashes cracked to her.

"I'm not stripping for me. I'm stripping for you, so I'd rather have you watch."

A large lump travelled through his throat. "Even if you're killing me, Karta?"

"Especially if I'm killing you, Dom."

He shook his head, his dark blue eyes opening wide to her.

Her skirt gone, she loosened the back of her short stays and flicked them off to the side of the bed.

Just her chemise left.

Her fingers light, she pushed one strap free from her shoulder, then the other. The silky cloth fell, catching against her curves as it dropped to folds about her feet.

He exhaled the longest, most agonized breath, and the quiver in his body deepened.

Naked, standing before him, his stare ravenous on her, she couldn't deny the fact that this was just as much torture for her. That she needed him deep inside her. Her folds were more than wet, more than ready for him. And she didn't know how much more willpower she had.

Sinking to her knees, she dropped forward to bury her hands into the bed along the outside of his thighs. She started to crawl up him, her face dipping low, her cheek rubbing along the tight, smooth skin of his shaft. Her mouth went down, her tongue flickering across the tip of him and then moving onto his lower abdomen. A circle with her tongue and she moved up his belly. Along the ridges of his muscles, tasting the salty sheen of sweat brimming across his body.

She craned her neck to look up at him, her eyes hooded. "How much more can you take, Dom?"

His wrists jerked against the bindings. Her knots held. "Don't ask me that—hell—I need you. I need you now, Karta."

The pain, the want, the carnal demand in his voice nearly did her in.

Instead, she managed to settle her legs on either side of his hips and she pulled herself upright. Wrapping her right hand about his member, she pulled it tall, settling the tip of it at her entrance.

He wanted to thrust upward. She could feel him—see him—fighting it. Fighting it with every muscle in his body.

This was all her decision and he wasn't about to take that away from her.

She put him out of his torture.

Sliding down onto him in one fluid motion, she took him deep, letting the width of him stretch her more than should have been possible.

A groan, still striving for control, erupted from his lips.

She lifted herself, then slid down him again, a panting scream bubbling from her own chest.

"Hell, Karta, faster."

She was already there. Lifting herself and descending in smooth strokes, his body slamming into hers, fast into the core of her. Over and over.

He lifted his hips from the bed, angling himself so every drive went deeper, grinding into the crux of her.

His groan turned into a roar, the sound twisting with the scream leaving her lips. Twisting with the pitch of her body as she slammed into him one last time, sending her over the precipice. She held tight, her body clasped fast to his, her hips twisting out of control with each brutal wave that took her, slamming her over the edge again and again.

His roar hit a pitch and his body writhed under her, lifting her high off the bed, the warmth from him a hot rush filling her deep.

She rode high, holding onto his waist as his body emptied into her, until he collapsed and sent them both crashing deep into the bed.

She landed on his chest with every muscle in her body trembling, her fingers searching for his skin, for something solid to hang onto in the throes of the wicked heaven swallowing her.

"Dammit, Karta, had I known that—hell—had I known that..." His words—from some far-off island—drifted to her.

With her head full, heavy with a thousand sparks of light, she could only manage to flip her chin flat onto his chest to look at him.

Wonderment in his dark blue eyes. Awe and lust and respect. All of it entwined in love.

Why had she even hesitated when she opened her eyes and saw him days ago in the drawing room below, rubbing her feet? Why had she even bothered with those moments of hate—hate she knew she could never hold to? Why had she resisted? Why had she not jumped on top of him then and there?

He'd always known what she needed. And she needed this.

He gave her equality in everything he was. He gave her everything he was—and with it, she could be everything she'd always hoped to be.

She buried her face into his chest for a long moment, inhaling the scent of his skin—sex and spice and sweat—and imprinted it in her mind, letting it spark to life the yearning in her core once more.

"Had you known that, what?" she asked.

"I would have murdered someone—anyone who stood between us—long ago just to live these last minutes with you."

She chuckled into his chest. "Then it is a good thing time unfolded as it did."

Her tongue slipped out, tasting him again. She wasn't done for the day—and she wasn't about to let him be either.

Wiggling up his naked body, she reached for one of the knotted strips of cloth, untying it. She moved to the other, repeating the process, then she hovered over him for a long breath. "Don't think you're done."

He laughed. "I wouldn't dream of it."

"Good, because I want you driving into me against the door next. And then on top of me, reaching into the very depths of me."

His laughter turned into a guttural growl and he sat upright, his hands curving along her backside and yanking her tight to his reawakened shaft. "I don't think Christmas will ever be the same."

She smiled as she leaned in, her nose brushing along his. "I don't think my life will ever be the same."

"Nor mine. This is the day it starts, Karta. The day right begins."

She nodded, her lips a feather against his. "Our right. Finally. A gift beyond all others."

His hand sank into the back of her hair, clasping her mouth to his in a toe-curling kiss.

Her smile, too big to contain, broke the kiss and he pulled slightly away. "What?"

"But you can still give me gifts," she said, mirth on her lips.

He chuckled, deep and warm. "The world, my lass. The world and more."

{ EPILOGUE }

Floorboards creaked next to her. Domnall's weight, sneaking out of the room again, leaving her to slumber in peace.

Just as he had every day for the last three months. Her head thick with sleep she was loath to leave, Karta opened her eyes and rolled onto her side—a feat of grand proportions with her belly as large as it was.

She looked about their bedroom. Her husband was nowhere in sight. He had been quick to escape this morning.

Then she saw it. A pink string.

A bright pink string, coming in through the door, weaving up over the sconce by the entrance, and then strung across the room to the foot of the bed.

Her toes wiggled. Something thick, stuck between her big and second toe.

The string was tied from her toe—or what she presumed was happening at the foot of the bed—she couldn't see her feet past her belly swollen so full with child she was sure her skin was going to burst open at any moment.

She wiggled her left big toe. The string moved. "Dom?"

No answer. He couldn't have gotten far, for she'd just heard him.

With a groan, she moved to sit up and swing her legs off the side of the bed. Once upright, the groan turned into a smile when she realized exactly what day it was.

And why she currently had a pink string tied to her toe. Christmas.

Leaning to the foot of the bed, she grabbed her wrap and pulled it about her shoulders. She bent over, stretching with her fingers to remove the string from her toe, but she couldn't reach her feet for her belly in the way.

She would just have to leave it.

With a heave, she pushed herself out of bed and waddled across the room. She lifted the thread from around the sconce and balled it in her hand as she followed it out into the hallway. Into the corridor and the string stopped at a table along the wall. The end of it tied to the foot of a large silver platter, and in the middle of the tray, a tiny marzipan bunny, sitting upright, front paws high, looking at her.

She laughed, looking around. "Dom?"

Silence.

Karta picked up the bunny, thinking for a moment to save it, but then she saw the blue string tied to the end baluster of the stairs three feet away. She popped the bunny into her mouth.

Heaven.

Bending her left leg up behind her, she managed to wedge her hand back far enough to tug the pink string free of her toe. Just as she set her foot down, Theodora bounded up the stairs, barking, her tail in a frenzy. She nuzzled into Karta's side, nudging her forward.

Karta laughed. "Hint received." She went to the blue string, her fingers pinching the thread as she followed it down the stairs.

An elephant in the drawing room was her reward at the end of the blue string.

She moved throughout the house with Theodora at her side, following entwined strings to and from rooms. Purple, teal, black, red, green, and yellow threads in a rainbow of gaiety guiding her to a penguin, a bear, a hawk, a squirrel, a deer, and a lion. All of them crafted with such fine attention to detail she was amazed by each creation.

At the lion in the kitchens, she paused again, looking around her. Not a soul was to be found anywhere she'd been in the abbey. "Dom?"

Still no answer.

She looked at the last thread tied to the leg of the table that she'd seen weaved amongst the others throughout the house, but hadn't yet gotten to the start of it. A gold thread. This was the start of it.

She moved to it, her forefinger and thumb pressing together to capture the silky string and she followed it.

The longest of all the threads, she followed it from room to room, up a level and back down a level until it delivered her to the study.

She pushed open the door. The golden thread stretched out across the room to a silver platter on the desk. Domnall was standing next to it, his dark blue eyes intent on her.

She laughed, running across the room as fast as her heavy belly would allow and she grabbed his arms. "I cannot believe you did this for me."

His eyes slightly squinted, trepidation tinging his look. "It was good?"

"It was beyond good—it was perfect." Her gaze dropped from her husband to the silver platter sitting next to him on the desk. In the center sat a grey…blob. She stared at it a long moment, trying to discern the shape of it. "But what? What is this one?" she asked, pointing at the platter.

He sighed with a quick shrug. "That one is a dog—Theodora, to be exact."

"Theodora?" She looked to the deerhound by their feet and then back to the marzipan candy. The color of it was the only resemblance to the dog. "It's…it's…"

"I made it. So it's not of the same quality as the others—far from it. Cook chuckled a few times as I tried to make it."

"You made it?"

He nodded.

"It's my favorite. I'm going to save this one." She picked it up, turning it in her fingers. There, a leg, maybe two. And maybe that was an ear perking up from the top. Her husband was not an artist. Yet it was perfect. Tears welled in her eyes.

"What? No—this wasn't supposed to make you cry." His thumbs lifted to her face, wiping her cheeks.

"No." She set the dog creation down and grabbed his wrists, stopping the motion. "It's perfect—so perfect that you did this—all of this—and it hurts my heart and then the tears just started. I'm happy—too happy." She'd only told him the story of what her grandmother did at Christmas once, but he had remembered every detail.

Of course he had. He always listened to her. He always had.

His eyebrows cocked. "So it's close enough to what your grandmother did? I wanted to attempt it before the babe is born, so I get it right for the both of you for the rest of our lives."

"It's just as grandmother did it." Her eyes went wide. "Except you sent me on the journey alone."

A sheepish smile quirked his mouth. "I didn't know if it would make ye happy or sad, so I didn't want to impose."

"It made me happy. Very, very happy." The brightest smile overtook her face, so brilliant her cheeks hurt.

"You're not lying to me?"

"I'm happy, more than you could ever know." Her hands clasped onto the sides of his face. "And do you remember last year how I got the best present ever—you?"

A flash of inordinate swagger crossed his dark blue eyes. "It is self-serving to say, but, yes. But I can say it only because I got you as my best present."

"I think I have an even better one for you this year."

"I already have ye, Karta. I can want for nothing else."

"Not even for this babe to arrive?"

"What? Now?" His jaw dropped, his look hardening on her. "Our babe? It is coming? Ye are positive?"

"I think I am. The pangs started once I got out of bed, just like the midwife described."

His eyes darkened, his mouth going to a terse line.

"Dom, you are not pleased?"

"Pleased?" He looked away from her, his jaw shifting back and forth for several long breaths.

A moment where she couldn't read what was in his eyes.

She set her palm to his cheek, tugging his face back toward her. "You are not pleased?"

His blue eyes suddenly softened, tears brimming in them. His mouth opened, his voice a rumbling whisper as he gently set his palms around the mound of her hard belly. "A babe. Our babe. How could I not be pleased? All of this, our life, is more than I ever could have hoped for."

His trunks of arms wrapped around her, encasing her fully, even with the extra girth of the babe.

Always protected. Always his.

Just as she'd always dreamed it could be.

~ About the Author ~

K.J. Jackson is the *USA Today* bestselling author of the *Hold Your Breath, Lords of Fate, Lords of Action, Revelry's Tempest, Valor of Vinehill, Box of Draupnir, Exile, Guardians of the Bones,* and *Creatures of Scales & Savagery* series.

She specializes in historical and paranormal fantasy romance, loves to travel (road trips are the best!), and is a sucker for a good story in any genre. She lives in Minnesota with her husband, two children, and a dog who has taken the sport of bed-hogging to new heights.

Visit her at www.kjjackson.com

~ Author's Note ~

Thank you for allowing my stories into your life and time—
it is an honor!

Be sure to check out all my historical romances
(each is a stand-alone story):

Hold Your Breath
Stone Devil Duke
Unmasking the Marquess
My Captain, My Earl

Lords of Fate
Worth of a Duke
Earl of Destiny
Marquess of Fortune

Lords of Action
Vow
Promise
Oath

Revelry's Tempest
Of Valor & Vice
Of Sin & Sanctuary
Of Risk & Redemption
To Capture a Rogue, *Logan's Legends*
To Capture a Warrior, *Logan's Legends*
The Devil in the Duke

Valor of Vinehill
The Iron Earl
The Wolf Duke
The Steel Rogue
The Christmas Countess
The Devil Baron

Box of Draupnir
The Heart of an Earl
The Blood of a Baron
The Soul of a Rogue

Exile
Exiled Duke
Wicked Exile
Dangerous Exile

Guardians of the Bones
Discreet Destruction
Shadows of Scandal
A Savage Deception
Wicked Reckoning

Paranormal Romance:
Creatures of Scales & Savagery
The Way You Break
Tear the World Down
Heathens in the Shadows
A Dynasty of Death

Contemporary Romance:
A Beautiful Average

Never miss a new release or sale!
Be sure to sign up for my VIP Email List at
www.KJJackson.com

Connect with me!
www.KJJackson.com ~or~ kjk19jackson@gmail.com

Printed in Great Britain
by Amazon

43884515R00078